DESERT CASCADE

The hours took their toll and as the silver half moon rose higher into the inky sky Shelter jerked and came alert. He had fallen asleep without realizing it. How many hours had passed? Too many.

There had been time for anyone to slip up behind him and merrily slit his throat.

Shell clawed his eyes open. It was a moment as he sat there sleep-drugged, his body feeling like a sack of stones before he realized that some one *had* been there.

The evidence was within arm's reach. A narrow-mouthed jug sat on the ground beside his leg, beside it was a small cloth-wrapped parcel.

Shelter picked up the jug. Water!

"Where in the hell did this come from?" he muttered.

"I have brought it to thee," came the voice of a woman, and Shell's head jerked around.

She stood there—moonlit, small and beautiful, her dark hair cascading down across her shoulders and breasts, her hands clasped at her waist, her white robe flowing along the lines of her body.

"Whoever you are," Shelter said eagerly, "I sure hope you're not a mirage!"

#12

SHELTER

BLOOD MESA
BY
PAUL
LEDD

ZEBRA BOOKS
KENSINGTON PUBLISHING CORP.

ZEBRA BOOKS

are published by

KENSINGTON PUBLISHING CORP.
475 Park Avenue South
New York, N.Y. 10016

Printed in the United States of America

1.

A high crimson cloud, like a curling dragon's tongue streaked the purple sundown skies. A broad, low mesa cut a stark silhouette against the sunset.

The hoofs of the shuffling gray mustang whished across the sand in the mesquite-thick river bottom. A rivulet of blood ran across the gray's muscular shoulder, trickling down from the hand of the man on its back.

The rider was a tall man with dark, shaggy hair and icy blue eyes. His dark blue shirt sleeve was ripped open and he had tied his red scarf tightly around the arm. The pain was an intense, throbbing ache. Just now he didn't have the time to worry about how much it hurt, whether that arrow wound was infected, when his horse might go down to stay.

He was worried about staying alive.

The Chiricahuas had risen up out of the sand and Shelter Morgan had tried to ride through them. Shoving his Colt into the face of the nearest Indian he had blown most of the warrior's head away and leaped the body with the gray.

He had heard a rifle bark then felt the jolting impact of an arrowhead, the searing following pain.

Morgan hadn't even looked back. He heeled the gray horse savagely and rode on, slumped over the withers, hearing the following shots.

"If I can make it until dark," he had told himself, "There's a chance."

It was nearly dark now, but it didn't look as if he was going to make it that long.

They were close behind him. The Apaches were afoot, but that was of no advantage to Shelter Morgan. Each time he looked back they were closer, jogging on steadily, methodically through the worst heat of the desert day.

Initially he had outdistanced them easily, but as the day wore on and the gray grew weary they closed the gap. Shelter had heard tell that an Apache—or any man in good condition—could eventually run down a horse. This was a hell of a time to have that notion proven accurate.

The gray was faltering badly as they climbed up out of the wash and onto the red sand flats. Shell could see almost nothing in the twilight. But they were there, their moccasins silent, their bodies only fleeting shadows in the wash. Or were they?

"Maybe I'm going mad with fever," Shell muttered. His arm felt swollen to twice its normal size and now, although it should have been cool as the sun died in the west, he felt as if he was burning up.

With difficulty he brought his Winchester repeater to his shoulder and fired two shots into the brush, trying to

6

slow them down a little. Two shots. No more. There weren't that many left and he would be needing them before long.

"Fighting shadows," he said to himself. Maybe he was going mad. Maybe the Apaches had long ago pulled off his trail. What in hell did he have that they wanted so badly? A rifle, a Colt handgun, a bowie, a half dead, leathery gray mustang, a blanket roll with a little jerky, some coffee, a couple of tins of peaches, a sack of flour.

"I killed one of 'em," he said. The horse hung its head. "I say that's why they want me, horse." He slapped the gray's neck and the horse shook its head. "I am feverish," he said. "Come on, jackass."

The horse plodded on, stumbling now from time to time, its flanks salt-flecked, quivering. The darkness was blanketing the land and skies. There was only a single, rounded reddish glow to mark the sunset. It haloed the jutting black mesa before Shelter, giving it an eerie aspect.

The horse stumbled and went down hard. Shelter hit the ground, landing on the injured shoulder and his eyes filled with tears as the searing pain shot through his body. The horse struggled to its feet and stood there shaking. Morgan stayed down.

He tried to get to his feet, but only got as far as hands and knees. He remained that way, his head spinning crazily, his eyes unfocused. He reached out, trying to find his Winchester, and fell again.

The gray stood looking down morosely at him.

Somewhere, and not far back there, were the Chiricahuas. "Damn it, Morgan!" he growled to the night, "get up!"

The spirit was willing, but that battered body just

7

wouldn't respond. Shell was bathed in sweat. The night was hot, hotter than hell. He gave it up, collapsed and rolled over onto his back, watching the stars blink on one by one above him.

There was still a faint glow, red and dull in the western sky, backlighting the hulking mesa. It would be enough. Enough light for them to find him by.

He managed to slide the Colt from his holster and prop himself up on one elbow. The Colt, cocked and loaded was in his hand.

The minutes passed with terrible slowness. The twin stars overhead began spinning crazily and Shelter had to blink away the image.

"Concussion," he said tonelessly. "Knocked away what little sense I had to begin with."

The gray's head came around and it stood, ears pricked, quivering, looking eastward, back toward the wash. They were coming.

Shell saw a darting shadow, heard the whisper of moccasins on sand. He wiped his eyes with his sleeve. The Colt was solid, heavy in his hand.

He could make out three of them now. They stood motionless, half-concealed by brush. They were waiting. Waiting for what? For the arrow wound to finish the job?

"Come on you bastards!" Shell shouted.

But they waited patiently, just out of decent handgun range. Shelter held his fire. He wanted to make his bullets count, wanted to take some of them with him.

He knew he'd had it. They always told him he'd get his one of these days, up some dark alley, alone on some miserable stretch of desert, in some hired woman's bed. He'd known it would happen, but he wished that he'd gotten Dabb first.

Lieutenant Horatio Dabb, formerly C.S.A. Former bastard. Former killer. That was something to live for—the pleasure of seeing Dabb die. Just now it looked like Shell would never have that pleasure.

The Apaches were all around him now. He could hear them in the brush, like small scuttling animals. They weren't troubling to be silent now. Why should they? They had their prey. They only had to wait.

They weren't that patient.

Shell saw someone creeping nearer, on his left hand side and he rolled over, panting and perspiring, his hand clenched around the butt of the big blue Colt.

"This is it," he thought. He heard one of them make a dash forward, moving up on the opposite side. His thumb was cramped over the hammer of the Colt.

Shell's eyes flickered that way and as they did he saw the Apache warrior on his left make his move. He turned his attention that way, raised the pistol and squeezed off.

The Apache was blown back ten feet, the bullet impacting high on his chest, tearing open a fist-sized hole where it exited.

Shelter rolled right, triggering off as the screaming Chiricahua hurled himself through the air, war ax held high. Shell fired again, spreading the Indian across the landscape. He folded up like a marionette with the strings cut and flopped to the earth, landing only three feet from where Shell lay.

The gray mustang whinnied in terror, went to its hind feet and took off at a run, reins dragging.

Three more. More cautious, these three warriors. They crept nearer, spreading like a fan. They wouldn't have been quite so cautious if they had known there were only two loads left in that Colt.

Any regrets, Morgan? Sure. There were dozens of laughing, bright eyed, full breasted, wide hipped women I never got to know. The day when I was finally, eventually going to lay down my guns and spend a year dozing in the sun, fishing up some lazy, sunny creek, never came. Hell, I wanted to see the sunrise tomorrow out on this desert, wanted to ride a fast-blooded horse across the distant plains, wanted to finish this job. This dirty, tedious, heartbreaking job.

"I wanted to kill Horatio Dabb," he said, speaking aloud without realizing it.

The Apaches were nearer now, still patiently stalking. Two bodies lay sprawled near Shelter. He could feel the warm sand beneath him, see the starlit sky, the approaching shadows.

He pulled back the hammer of his Colt again and lifted his arm. They halted.

Shelter blinked. His head was beginning to spin again. There seemed to be a mass of stars behind the Indians. They seemed to lift their arms and chant. He blinked again.

They were backing away and Shelter couldn't figure it.

They had him and they knew it. Two of their number might have been down, but that wasn't going to stop the Apaches from finishing what they'd started.

"It's a trick," he told himself, not convinced somehow of what he said.

He knew, somehow knew that there was someone behind him and he spun, going prone, Colt uplifted and ready. He never fired.

It was madness. The fever had finally gotten to his brain. That gnawing pain had destroyed his reason. There before him stood a woman, but a woman such as he had never seen, had no reason to expect to see out on this wild and barren desert.

She stood in the starlight, her long dark hair curling across her shoulders, dressed in a long white gown. Her eyes were luminous and wide. She stood with arms upraised, looking not at Shelter, but at the wash beyond where the Indians had been.

Or maybe nowhere, at nothing. The look was far away, unreadable.

Shell tried to speak, to say anything, to ask a question, but when he looked again the vision was gone. He looked left and right; then, figuring he was in the middle of a pain-inspired delusion, he rolled back to face the Apaches. Gone! The night was as still and silent as on the morning after Creation.

It was too much. He had no explanation, was not sure if it was illusion or truth. He propped himself up again but he didn't last long. The loss of blood, the shock, the deprivation had taken their toll and although he knew he *had* to stay alert, had to be ready for them when they came again, he just couldn't make it, couldn't will that body of his to stay vigilant and he slumped over onto his face, the gun falling from his hand, knowing that he would never see the next sunrise, knowing that they would come in the night and finish the job. It somehow didn't matter. Not anymore.

The trail had ended. Short of Dabb, Lieutenant, C.S.A. Well, it had to end sometime. It couldn't be as endless as it had seemed all these years.

It stretched a long way back, this murderous, bitter trail, all the way back to Georgia, all the way back to that great war which had torn a nation apart, destroyed thousands upon thousands of lives, set Shelter Morgan upon this vengeance trail.

"Captain Morgan?"

Shelter opened his eyes. He was exhausted, hungry, worn to nerve ends. He rested in a cannon-blackened grove along the Conasauga River in Georgia. The Bloody Conasauga they called it. The river ran red after a month's fighting. The Union forces were gradually squeezing them. The food had run out; there were no blankets and damned little ammunition. Men walked barefoot into battle. The fever was raging. Soldiers lay screaming in the night as the surgeon, without anesthetics, amputated limbs.

"What is it?" Morgan asked.

"Colonel would like to see you, sir."

"All right."

Shelter Morgan struggled to his feet and walked toward the colonel's tent, noticing the fresh horses being held by an enlisted man beside the tent. He rapped on the tent frame and was summoned.

They sat there looking up at him from a makeshift table. Colonel Fainer, Morgan's commanding officer, Major Twyner, Captain Reg Bowlen, who was a secret hoarder, Gordon Wakefield, Lieutenant Horatio Dabb, a neat, aesthetic appearing man with calm blue eyes, wavy blond hair and a patrician nose. In the shadows sat another man of high rank. The lamplight shone on the silver star of a brigadier general. General Custis, known up and down the line for his tactical genius. He had been at Lookout Mountain up near Chickamauga and had defended Chatsworth against Sherman with a dozen cannon and plenty of bluff.

"Sir," Morgan saluted and was asked to take a seat. It was the general who did most of the talking.

12

"You're a Tennessee man."

"Yes, sir. From Pikeville."

"That's near to Chickamauga."

"A stone's throw," Morgan replied.

"We were run out of Tennessee, Morgan. It was a bitter defeat at Chickamauga."

"Yes, sir."

"Do you know Lookout Mountain?"

"I've hunted there. I know it."

"Home country, heh?" the general smiled. Shelter looked at Colonel Fainer who nodded.

"Yes, sir. I've wandered those hills."

"Know all the backtrails, the ridge routes, do you?"

"I know them as well as any man," Shell said, curiosity mounting.

"I see." Custis was silent. He and Fainer exchanged a glance.

"He's the man, sir," Colonel Fainer said softly.

"Yes, I believe he is," Custis responded. He sighed. "All right, Morgan, I'll tell you what this is about. When we pulled out of Tennessee, we pulled out in a hurry. We left much behind."

"Yes, sir, I know that."

"Do you, I wonder?" Custis said enigmatically. "I'll tell you exactly what we left, sir! A quarter of a million dollars in gold! A payroll bound for Lee's army. It never got through. We had to get the hell out."

"A quarter . . ."

"You heard me, sir," the general snapped. "A quarter of a million in gold. Have you any idea how much that is translated into medical supplies, musket balls, blankets and shoes?" Custis leaned nearer, the lanternlight shining in his green eyes. "We need that gold, sir. We've got

13

contacts, British merchants ready to supply us with all we need to survive this winter, to hopefully prolong this war just a little while, to build some bargaining strength, to feed our people, to keep a thousand more from dying of pneumonia!''

"You want me to have a try at recovering it," Shelter Morgan said.

Custis looked at Shell, chewing on his lower lip thoughtfully. "Yes, sir. That is exactly it. We needed a man who knows that country like his own backyard. We needed a man of scrupulous honesty, a man of determination. Colonel Fainer tells me that you are all of these.''

"I appreciate the compliment."

"It had better be more than a compliment, sir!'' the general said. "You had better be exactly what the colonel believes you to be. I can't begin to tell you how much depends on this.''

Shelter had taken the assignment. A fool's mission, it was. Sift through the Union lines, recover the gold which Custis and his fellow officers had hidden, return through enemy positions without being captured or killed.

But they had made it. Keeping to the high ridges, travelling only at night, Shelter had led his hand-picked squad through the Northern lines and into Tennessee. Luck was with them and they found the hidden gold, plucking it practically from beneath Union eyes.

They lost one man on the way back. One who had been told to keep down and didn't listen. But by God, they had made it!

Captain Shelter Morgan, Sergeant Jeb Thornton, Welton Williams who was too good with guns for his own good, and bespectacled Private Dinkum, known as the Dink—they had done it and they were rejoicing in it.

14

They, by God, had beat the odds, beat the whole damned Union army.

They came upon the others in a clearing.

They were all there. General Custis, Colonel Fainer, Twyner, Captain Bowlen, Horatio Dabb looking as calm and neat as ever, Leland Mason. Twenty men in all, officers and enlisted. They were all wearing civilian clothes.

Shelter's men had reined up, the horses shifting nervously, perhaps sensing something. Shell looked at Custis who was resplendent in a white linen suit, and asked "War over, is it, General?"

"It's been over for a long time, Captain Morgan," Custis answered. "Anyone with eyes to see could tell you that. We've gotten our butts whipped."

"It's time to get out then," Shelter said. His eyes shifted from man to man. He was seeing the determination in their eyes. He was remembering each one, feeling it now.

"They want the gold," Welton Williams said and Shelter looked at the dark eyed gun hawk.

"Is that right?" Morgan asked.

"Shelter," Colonel Fainer said, "the war is over. It's like the general says, it's ended. In a few months we'll all be surrendering our weapons. And then what? We'll go home to our burned houses, home to places where we won't even be able to vote or have a voice in our destinies. The South is dead, boy! We've fought for a just cause. Well, the cause is lost. Let us have something for the price we've paid. Let us go west or across the seas, let us start again!"

"With this gold?"

"That's it."

"That's what we went through hell for? To deliver this

15

gold to you—officers who are going to desert your men! No, we took an oath, gentlemen. Maybe you don't recall it, but I damned sure do. Not only that, what you told me was true—we have hundreds who need this gold for medical supplies, for blankets, for food. I'll not hand it over, sir.''

"Shell, son, you have no choice," Colonel Fainer said, swallowing hard and Morgan simply stared at him. Fainer who had been his friend, his commanding officer, the man Morgan admired most in this world.

"Don't," Morgan had told them.

"There's twenty of us."

"I don't give a damn if there's a hundred, sir."

A horse blew, a crow croaked in a blackened oak tree. Shell's mouth was dry. Then it happened.

Afterward he was never sure who had started it—probably Welton Williams who lived through it to become a crippled, savage man. Williams who fought with two guns and seldom missed what he shot at—until that other day when he tried Shelter Morgan on for size.

The guns exploded in the silence of the day. Gunsmoke rolled across the clearing. Horses went down in a thrashing, bloody heap. Jeb Thornton, beside Shell, was blown from the saddle. An injured bay horse did a dance on Welton Williams' chest, crushing him. Dinkum caught a bullet in the face, another in the shoulder and Shelter told him, "Run!"

Dinkum had while Shell held them back for a fragment of a minute with his own sidearm, before he himself was tagged and he rode out of the ring of death clinging to the mane of the big horse he rode while the bullets whined all around him, while the gunsmoke burned his nostrils and hot blood trickled out of his wounded body.

Later he had found the Dink dead. Later still the boys in the blue uniforms had found Captain Morgan, still living, but barely. They had patched him up and thrown him into prison on spy charges.

And that prison. It was not so bad as Andersonville, perhaps, but not much better. The war ended and Shell was still a prisoner. Lee went free and still Morgan was held.

There were seven long years of that. He had been captured in the civilian clothes he had worn to slip through the Union lines and so they had sentenced him as a spy. Their questioning proved that they thought he knew something about a large amount of gold missing at war's end. Shell always believed that someone had informed, wanting to keep him in that prison for as long as possible. Because they knew.

They knew that when Shelter Morgan was free nothing in this world could keep him from coming after them. They had killed three in that clearing that day. They had killed hundreds of others—those who froze that winter, those who starved or died of the lack of medical supplies.

These men, these trusted leaders had grabbed what they could and run. They had taken an oath, but it meant nothing to them.

Shelter Morgan had taken another kind of oath that day he had stepped out of the Maryland prison into the sunlight. He would run them down and they would pay. Nothing could break that oath. Nothing but Morgan's own death.

2.

The sun was low, red, in a deep blue sky. Dove flew low across the desert flats, a scrub jay called from the wash.

Shelter Morgan rolled over with a groan then he sat up sharply, too sharply. His head began to spin. His stomach turned over once.

He sat there, head in hands, looking at the patch of sand beneath him. Then slowly he glanced around, reaching first for the Colt which still lay beside him.

He picked it up and frowned. The weight was wrong. Spinning the cylinder he discovered why. The gun had been emptied. He looked around but failed to find the bullets. His gunbelt loops were empty.

"What in bloody hell . . ." Shell struggled to his feet, the attempt sending a surge of fresh pain through his arm. He glanced at the arm and muttered another oath.

Someone had bandaged the arm!

He looked twice, blinked and shook his head, peering toward the rising sun. The Indians were gone. There was no sign of the dead.

If it hadn't been for the bandage Shelter would have thought he had taken too much sun and was suffering some strange delusion. The bandage and the gun.

"Christ."

He staggered to the meager shade of a mesquite bush and sat down staring at the empty desert, the hulking red mesa. "What in hell is going on?"

There had been a fight. He had nailed two Indians within fifty feet of where he now sat. The Indians were gone. Someone had bandaged his arm but emptied his gun. He frowned. Why hadn't the Apaches killed him? Why would they empty his gun? They damn sure wouldn't bandage him up.

The memory, fragmented and blurred, returned to him.

The memory of a dark haired woman in a long white robe standing behind him as the Apaches made their last attack. But that couldn't have been real. Where in hell would she have come from? She certainly hadn't held back the Apaches alone.

"Saying it is possible, saying she is the one who bandaged me, why help me and then empty my gun and leave me lying here?"

The desert had no answer. A stream of red ants flowed past, clambering over the mesquite beans, rushing in a zig-zag line across the coarse grained sand to an anthill mound. The jay called again from the wash and Shelter Morgan got to his feet.

"What now, Morgan?" he asked himself. He stood, thumb hooked into his gunbelt, searching the empty land.

19

Nothing. Beyond the wash a long stretch of red sand desert, distant conical hills of volcanic origin, empty white playas baked by the sun—dead lakes of another time.

In the other direction was the massive mesa, maybe a thousand feet high, perhaps twenty miles around. Far beyond that was the town of Delgado, the town Shelter had been heading for when the Chiricahua hit him.

He had an appointment with a man living there.

Horatio Dabb.

The ex-Confederate soldier had approached Shell in Safford while Shell was at his supper. The ex-soldier had been watching Morgan for some time. He was scrawny with sad brown eyes, a beard too gray for his age, narrow shouldered, hollow chested. He coughed violently from time to time.

Finally he had gotten up from his own table and walked across the restaurant to stand opposite Shell.

"Ain't you Captain Morgan."

"I am," Shell answered a little warily.

"Thought so. Richmond Plovers," the soldier said, sticking out a gnarled hand.

"Have some coffee?" Shell gestured toward the stone pot the waitress had brought with his meal.

"Thank you, sir, I will."

Plovers snatched a cup from a nearby table and poured himself some coffee. "What can I do for you?"

"What I hear, you've already done something for me."

"Oh?"

"Don't worry, I ain't gonna talk about it here. But words gets around, sir. Us old Rebs kind of stick together out here. I used to have a hell of a lot of enemies, you see. Thing is, one by one they kind of seem to be dying off."

Morgan didn't answer. He finished up his bacon and beans and tilted back, waiting for Plovers to say what he had come to say.

"There's another old Reb living not far from here," Plovers said finally. "Man name of Horatio Dabb. At least that was once his name. He's changed it now. Calls himself Charles Dantworth."

"It's always nice to know where old friends are," Shell replied casually.

"It surely is. Lieutenant Dabb now, he's over west in a place called Delgado. Reason I know is he came here one day with a bunch of hard men, picked up some kind of shipment from the railroad terminal and left. I was watching him, just wishing . . ."

"You know much about Dabb?"

"Not now." Plovers shook his head. "But I know all about what he *was*. I wanted to kill him," Plovers said, his voice loud in the restaurant. Heads turned toward their table.

"Why didn't you?"

"It ain't all that easy," Plovers said. He thumped his right arm up onto the table and Shell saw the hand was gone.

"They took that off with no ether, no whiskey. Nothing but a nice sharp saw. I was lucky. I made it. But it surely does make it difficult to do some of the jobs a man would like to do for himself." Plovers rose abruptly. "Been nice talking to you, Morgan. You get the chance, you look up our mutual friend, hear?"

Shelter Morgan doubted just now that he was going to be looking up anyone real soon.

He wiped back his shaggy dark hair and frowned. The sun was a fierce white ball in the empty sky. The desert heat was returning. Nothing visible stirred out on the flats. The snakes were curled up in their shady spots, the coyotes in their dens.

Shell slowly circled the clearing, trying to read the sign. No, he wasn't completely mad—there were the vague imprints of Indian moccasins, the semi-boots the Apaches favored. Here he could see where a man had been dragged into the brush, and crouching he found the maroon stains on the sand. Drying blood.

Walking westward fifty paces he found the other foot-prints.

Small bare feet, indistinct in the soft sand.

"Be damned," Shell muttered, rising out of his crouch. "A lone young woman, walking around bare-foot." Out here!

That made it certain that she hadn't come from far away. No one could walk barefoot in this country where the sand reached a hundred and fifty degrees and more, where the ground was littered with cactus spines, where scorpions and snakes lay in unsuspected places, where the sand was broken by glassy volcanic rock sharp enough to cut a boot or a horse's hoofs to ribbons.

Shell looked around and grunted with satisfaction. He had spotted his Stetson lying crumpled and dusty beneath a clump of sage. He walked to it, picked it up, dusted and formed it and put it on his head.

The second surprise was even better. His Winchester, all but buried in the sand, lay nearby. He picked it up noting as he jacked a cartridge through that it at least had not been unloaded.

The needle gun was .44-40, the exact cartridge his Colt took—that was one of the reason for buying that caliber weapon, the cartridges were interchangeable. Shell flicked the lever five times, picked up the brass cartridges the Winchester had spit out, and loaded his handgun.

Then he began walking.

The sun seemed to be focused on a point between his shoulder blades. The wind was dry off the mesa. His arm throbbed and he was thirsty. He needed to find that mustang. He needed both the horse and the water in the canteen hanging from the saddlehorn if he was going to make it out of this country.

And out was where he wanted to be.

The Chiricahua were still around somewhere. Somehow through some fluke Shell didn't understand, they had let him live last night. He could hardly count on a second escape.

He felt better about things with the loaded Colt and the Winchester which still had four cartridges, but he would have felt a damn sight better with a horse between his legs.

He found its tracks a quarter of a mile on.

There was no doubt that it was his horse. The gray had a specially made built-up right hind shoe. The horse was walking slowly, wandering across the sand, pausing from time to time to nibble at the mesquite bushes and the yucca.

It was moving toward the mesa and Shelter walked that way through the heat of the day, his boots sinking into the soft sand, the sun doing its best to bore a hole through the top of his skull.

The white man loomed up out of the sand directly in front of Morgan.

White he was. Pale skinned, white bearded with a long white beard. He was wearing a white robe over his thin frame.

He was there, hand lifted to the skies, his eyes expressionless, and then he was gone.

Simply gone.

Shell rushed up the low sandy knoll and looked around meticulously. There was no sign of the old man. He shook his head. What in hell was this? Concussion, heat exhaustion, mirage?

First the girl and then this old man, rising like a prophet out of the sands. Shelter heard the horse whicker from nearby and he forgot about the old man. He was going to climb aboard that mustang and get the hell out of here. Let the spirits have this desert. Spirits, ghosts, mirages, whatever they were. They sure as hell weren't living flesh and blood people. They couldn't be.

Out here where nothing grew, this waterless land overrun by hostile Apaches?

Shelter found the horse looking mournful and weary, its saddle slipped sideways, standing in a brushy thicket in the shadow of the great mesa which towered over them.

Even in the shade the day was incredibly hot, incredibly dry. Shelter cursed as he saw that somewhere the gray had lost the canteen. The saddle, tilting to the side had allowed the canteen strap to slip from the saddlehorn.

Shell loosened the cinches, removed the saddle long enough to rub the gray's back with the blanket, then refolded the blanket, smoothed it and saddled up again. He had to find that canteen. His body was already protesting the lack of moisture and it was twenty miles across the desert to Delgado.

Stepping into leather, Shell shoved the Winchester into the saddle boot and began backtracking.

The gray was beat, but seemed pleased to have guid-

once again, and it stepped out along the foot of the mesa as Shell searched for the canteen.

There was a small rustling sound like that of a rattler on the prod and Shelter jerked around in time to see the Apache come up out of the brush and leap at him, knife in hand.

Morgan kicked free of the stirrup and planted his boot squarely in the Indian's face. His nose exploded with blood and he fell face down into the sand, his knife tearing away a part of Shell's pant leg.

The second one fired from the cover of a stack of reddish boulders along the foot of the mesa. His first shot missed, but not by much. It struck the cantle of Shell's saddle and whined off into the distance, an angry, spinning chunk of metal.

Shell went low behind the gray's shoulder and cut loose an unaimed shot which missed wide, burying itself in the face of the mesa. The Indian fired again and Shell felt the gray buckle at the knees, felt the big mustang recover and then start to go down.

He threw himself free, grabbing for the Winchester, feeling it slide through his fingertips as he hit the superheated sand in a diving roll, as the gray, whinnying pitifully landed on its back and waved its flailing hoofs in the air, blood spattering the sand around it.

Shell was up and running, bullets singing around him. He dove into the clump of scrub oak and manzanita brush at the base of mesa, the bullets from the Apache rifles clipping branches all around him.

Shell ducked low, squirmed to one side and cautiously lifted his head. The Apache and Morgan touched off at the same moment. Neither hit anything, but the Apache's shot was close enough to cause Shell to sweat.

The Indian, or Indians—he had no way of knowing how many there were—had better cover behind those rocks. In time one of the searching bullets would find Morgan where he lay sweltering in the brushy thicket.

He had to move and move now.

Where was a whole 'nother question.

Morgan looked around, seeing only the spread of sandy desert before him, the rising fluted walls of the vast mesa behind him. Another bullet drove him to his belly and he angrily triggered off a shot, sending a precious bullet ricocheting off the boulders where the Apaches were concealed.

That might breed caution momentarily, but it wouldn't hold them back for long.

Shell swivelled his head, looking for an escape route, finding none. Sweat stung his eyes and trickled down his spine. His shoulder ached heavily. Someone seemed to be pounding it methodically with a twelve-pound sledge hammer. The brilliant sun clawed at his eyes.

He saw an Apache make a dash toward the boulders, followed him with the muzzle of his Colt and cut loose. The Apache crumpled up and then dragged himself out of Shelter's line of sight, a bloody leg following.

Moments later three rifles opened up from that position. Help had arrived.

Shell looked eastward once again. Nothing moved out on the desert. The gray horse lay dead in a pool of black blood. "All right, Morgan, suck it up," Shell told himself. He didn't like it, but there was no choice—he had to make a run for it.

He eased back, moving as cautiously and quietly as possible toward the base of the mesa. Brush scratched at his face and hands. He saw a sidewinder slither away, saw a shadow move as an Indian shifted position.

Slowly he gathered himself, drawing his legs up under him, staying low. Then he fired two shots from the Colt and took off at a dead run, staying in a crouch as the bullets from the Apache position sang off the rock around and behind him.

He ran a hundred yards, the useless Colt in his hand, his breath coming in short, ragged gasps. Suddenly the canyon mouth yawned before him.

Shelter automatically turned up it. There was no cover at all out on the flats. This was something. A chance.

He quickly discovered it wasn't much of a canyon. Simply a narrow cleft cut by running water over the eons in the caprock of the mesa. The canyon narrowed quickly and rose steeply.

Shell scrambled up it, clambering over loose rock and litter left by flash floods. An Apache rifle barked again and Shelter hit the earth. He lay there panting for a long minute then turned cautiously and looked down the slope of the canyon to the mouth of the cut.

They were gone again, damn them. It was like fighting shadows. These men knew this country, knew the ways of war. They didn't hold their positions long and when they moved it was with swift, calculated precision.

The day before they had gotten Shelter with one of the oldest, most effective tricks in the Apache war manual. Lying in scooped out hollows in the sand they had covered themselves, leaving only room to see, to breathe. It was impossible to detect them; it was impossible to understand how they could endure it, but the Apache was long on endurance.

Shell had fought the Apache before and he both admired and despised him; feared and respected him. The

Apache was a savage, brutal breed, but by God, he was a fighting man!

They were up to something now, and Morgan couldn't figure it. He didn't want to wait and find out what they had in mind, and so he decided to break it up a little.

He moved behind one of the bigger boulders which were strewn along the canyon's tilting floor and sat down. Back against the ground, he lifted his boots to the rock and shoved.

Nothing happened.

He tried again, shoving until his legs ached and his back popped. Finally he felt the rock tilt up off its moorings, felt it begin to slowly roll over, gathering momentum.

Shell scooted behind another boulder and watched. The big rock increased its speed, hit a small rock and bounded high into the air, carrying a shower of smaller, head-sized boulders in its wake.

Shell heard an Apache yell, saw the landslide build, developing into a wave of earth and rock. Stone pinged off stone, rumbled down the long slope. Shelter saw the Apaches make a run for it, saw one crushed beneath the big boulder.

Then he turned and scrambled on, moving upslope. They would be back. They would keep coming back until they had his scalp hanging from their leggings.

Shell climbed up the sloping canyon floor, moving toward the caprock high above. The sun, coasting overhead erased the shadows cast by the canyon walls and it became a furnace in the cleft. No breeze stirred. Sweat rained off of Shelter Morgan. His head ached dully. He looked behind him constantly, but he saw the Apaches no more. No matter, they would find him again. They had

28

him and they knew it. How in hell was he supposed to get off this mesa and travel the twenty miles to the nearest settlement across searing desert, weaponless, without water or a horse?

Answer—he wasn't.

He was going to sit on this mesa until he starved or died of thirst, until the Apaches made up their minds to slip up and skin him. It was damned near enough to make a man sit down, quit, wait for them.

Morgan wasn't that kind of man.

Looking up he could see the caprock, see a dozen cedar trees growing along the rim. That gave him some hope of finding water, but it was a faint hope. Deer, maybe? If so he might be able to eat, to drink, to hold out for a time.

Assuming the Apaches didn't come.

But they would. Through the heat of the day, or flitting softly through the canyon one silent night. Shelter had killed some of them, wounded others. He had become a formidable warrior in their eyes. One worth the hunting, one worthy of a long, slow, painful warrior's death.

3.

It was late afternoon before Shelter, breathing heavily from his climb, emerged onto the caprock of the mesa and stood there, hands on hips, chest rising and falling rapidly, surveying the land around him.

It was mostly flat, with here and there sinks where water had broken through the primeval caprock, with a few upthrust, convoluted hills along the western edge. There was some grass, quite a few cedars, and here and there a scraggly stand of spruce.

Shelter's tongue was sticking to his palate. His throat was so dry it seemed barely open. He was trembling from the exertion. His face was flushed and dry. His clothing was plastered to his body.

He needed to find water, if water there was to be found, but he did not turn away from the canyon. He sat down, breathing in deeply. A dry, twisting breeze ran across the mesa, heating his body more than it cooled it.

He sat and he looked down the water-cut gorge, watching for the Apaches, wondering if there was another way up, where it was.

Shelter remained there for over an hour. Then deciding that they weren't coming, not then, not that way, he rose stiffly and began his search of the mesa.

He kicked a cottontail out of the high grass and it scotted away, zig-zagging, bounding. Shell watched it hungrily. He carried an empty Colt and a bowie knife. If he was to eat he would have to fashion snares, dead-falls, game traps. Perhaps he would make a bow and some arrows.

He decided he definitely would after seeing the droppings of a mule deer. The thought of roast venison made his stomach tighten and growl.

Shelter walked to the very edge of the mesa rim and stood looking out into the vast distances. The desert was blued by the shimmering heat veils, the far hills brown and partly shadowed. A mirage lake glittered in the sun, shifting, taunting.

Shelter turned away, tugging his hat down over his eyes against the sun. He went back to the canyon mouth and hunkered down, searching for any sign of the Apaches, but there was none. Although he remained there for over an hour this time he saw nothing, heard only the emptiness and the low keening of the dry wind. They had chosen not to follow and it worried Shelter.

By this time his body was crying out for water. His mouth seemed to be filled with hot dry sand. He set out in search of a water hole, a sink, a spring.

He worked his way through the cedars, knowing that they were drawing water from somewhere. Of course the

31

source could be far underground, or perhaps they just hung on between rare desert rains. The trees were ancient but not tall. Wind-flagged and gnarled.

Emerging from the trees Shell looked westward again, seeing the odd, upthrust, ridgebacked hills there. Remnants of some ancient time, carrying the memories of the eons, they had been thrust up by internal pressures before time had begun, before the thousands of uncounted centuries had washed away the land surrounding the mesa, leaving only the mesa, protected by its caprock to stand above the ancient, dry sea which was the desert.

Shelter walked that way. The air was dry, carrying the scent of cedars, of sun-baked grass. The ridgebacked hills rose up before him, dark, basaltic, primitive.

Shell noticed the dark streak against the earth and he walked to it, crouching down. The ground was damp. Water had leaked down—or was seeping up—sometime during the last twenty-four hours. That suggested a spring and Morgan walked on.

He moved upslope now, through the tilted, narrow spinelike rocks. They were arranged in nature's random order, but somehow these rocks, most of them twenty feet high, a few feet thick, gave the impression of having been arranged by intelligence. It was like walking through a giant graveyard past dark tombstones which marked the graves of titans.

He could not find the source of the water. He searched upslope to the south and then back downslope and north. The tombstones cast long shadows now as the sun sank in the west.

Shell trudged on.

His leg suddenly went out from under him. His boot sank into the earth to mid calf. He nearly snapped his an-

32

kle and he steadied himself, muttering a curse.

He crouched down examining the sinkhole or whatever it was. He scooped out some of the earth and held it up in puzzlement.

Sand.

He looked around, mystified. This was the oldest part of the mesa, and the mesa itself was millions of years older than the surrounding desert. All around Shell was decaying basalt, slate, primeval granite.

Where in hell could the sand have come from?

It might—might—have blown up from below. A small quantity of it, but it sure as hell didn't fly up and bury itself in this sinkhole.

It could, he conjectured, be pushed up from far below by a spring. He dug a little deeper, searching for dampness. Carefully he scooped the sand up and placed it aside. As he dug the sides of the hole collapsed, forming a new shape.

The edge of the hole was nearly straight, Shell noticed. He was encouraged by that. There might have once been an ancient well here.

He went down three feet before his hand found something solid and smooth beneath the sand. Shell gave a yank and as his hand came up he found himself holding a human bone.

The femur, the thighbone of a man. Or a woman. It seemed to Shell to be awfully long for the short Indians living around here now, but then he knew next to nothing about such things and he shoved that thought aside.

He crouched back on his heels, hat tilted up, the bone in his hands. He hadn't found a well, but a burial site. He started to flip the bone back into the hole he had excavated, but some vague curiosity caused him to place the bone aside and dig a little deeper.

The shadows were gathering rapidly now, the pools of darkness settling around the bases of the tombstones which now seemed more than ever to deserve being termed that.

Shell's fingers hooked a ribcage and he brought it up in pieces. Searching, he found the skull. He held it up, turning it in the purpling light of late afternoon. Something seemed wrong about the skull, but he couldn't put his finger on it.

He dug a little deeper.

It was round, smooth, small, and when he pulled it out of the sand it gleamed in the dusky sunlight.

A twenty-dollar gold piece. Minted in 1870 at Carson City.

"How in hell . . ." Shell dug some more. What was that nearly new double eagle doing in this place? The grave obviously was not ancient as Shell had imagined. Whoever was buried here had died in the last seven years and been planted with a double eagle. Or—someone had excavated the grave and left the coin behind. Maybe it had fallen from someone's pocket. But then who in hell would want to dig up an old grave?

His fingers found the clay pot and he pulled it up. It was the size of Shelter's head, made crudely of unfired red clay, the edges pinched like a piecrust, a few unskillfully drawn symbols scratched into it.

And it was brim full of gold!

Eagles, double-eagles and below that pounds of silver dollars all recently minted.

Shell sat dazed, looking at the pot. Even figuring the bottom layer to be silver money, there was close to five thousand dollars in the clay pot. Buried here on top of an

34

inaccessible mesa in the middle of a godforsaken desert in an unmarked grave.

"Figure that one out, Morgan," he muttered.

He didn't have time to do any figuring. The arrow struck the rock beside his head and Shelter dove to the side, rolling until he was behind another tilted tombstone.

The gold was spilled across the earth to gleam dully in the late sunlight. The bones lay stacked beside the grave. Shell pulled his bowie from its sheath and crouched low, ready.

He heard footsteps to his right and began to circle left, moving as soundlessly as possible, placing his boots carefully, toe first, then heel.

He froze.

He saw his adversary moving toward the tombstone, arrow notched, ready. Shelter pressed himself against the shadowed stone at his back, his chest rising and falling rapidly. Placing his hat on the ground he peered around the tombstone and then crept forward, bowie held low, blade upturned.

A stone rolled under his foot and Shelter groaned inwardly. His prey turned, fired an arrow wildly and then made a mad dash for safety.

Shelter was on his heels. He lunged for his man, missed and recovered. He saw the man vanish behind a tombstone and rushed after him. Shell forced himself to slow slightly, not knowing who or what was behind the stone.

Cautiously he moved around the giant slab of basalt. The shadows were heavy, pooling at his feet, the sun was a rosy memory in the western skies.

Nothing.

There was no one there, not a footprint. Shell worked

his way forward, walking through the graveyard of the titans.

Nothing.

He was gone, vanished like the wind. Shell gave it up, sheathed his bowie and walked back toward the open grave. The arrow lay there, shattered, and Shell picked it up, grunting as he examined it.

It had a steel arrowhead.

But then he had already known the man who attacked him was not Apache. Very few Apaches roamed around wearing long white robes.

He kicked the bones and the gold back into the grave and covered them with sand. He recovered his hat and began making his way out of the graveyard, moving cautiously through the dusk.

The mesa had suddenly ceased to become a refuge. There were people up here every bit as dangerous as the Apaches down on the desert. And every bit as elusive.

None of it made any sense. Barefoot maidens in white robes, old patriarchs in flowing beards, graves full of gold, mysterious assassins. Again he wondered if he wasn't suffering from some strange delusion.

But there was always the bandage. Someone had tended that arm, wrapped it in clean linen. Someone had emptied his pistol . . . it was too tangled and Shell could make no sense of it.

He had found no water, found no sanctuary. He was in worse shape than he had been that morning. He was out of ammunition, out of water and damned near out of his mind.

He returned through the cedar woods to the mouth of the canyon. Sagging to the earth, propped up against a red, rough boulder, he watched the trail, waiting for them to come, his eyes blurry and heavy, his face haggard, his body slowly weakening, his mind vast confusion.

The hours took their toll and as the silver half moon rose higher into the inky sky Shelter jerked and came alert. He had fallen asleep without realizing it. How many hours had passed? Too many.

There had been time for anyone to slip up behind him and merrily slit his throat.

Shell clawed his eyes open. It was a moment as he sat there sleep-drugged, his body feeling like a sack of stones before he realized that some one *had* been there.

The evidence was within arm's reach. A narrow-mouthed jug sat on the ground beside his leg, beside it was a small cloth-wrapped parcel.

Shelter picked up the jug. Water!

Lord, it was sweet and cool. It flowed across his tongue like icy silver honey and his body came alert, demanding more as it trickled down his throat and into his stunned, greedy stomach.

He drank just a few sips though all of his cells cried out for more, demanded that he glut himself, drink pint after pint of the saving liquid.

Shell opened the parcel and found that it contained cheese and biscuits. He frowned.

"Where in the hell did this come from?" he muttered.

"I have brought it to thee," she said and Shell's head jerked around.

She stood there—moonlit, small and beautiful, her dark hair cascading down across her shoulders and breasts, her hands clasped at her waist, her white robe flowing along the lines of her body.

This time she did not run.

Morgan got to his feet slowly, stiffly, and she held her

37

ground, watching him with wide, gentle eyes.

"You brought this to me?" he asked.

"Yes. It was I."

"But why?"

"Why?" She smiled softly. "Because thou wert without."

She was utterly beautiful. The silver moon highlighted her black, silky hair. Her eyes, childlike and yet wise were wide, dark, still. "I'm dreaming," Shell thought.

"Drink thy fill," she said. "Please."

Shell sat again, first looking around to see who else might be watching him. He saw no one, heard nothing and so he did as she suggested, sipping the cool water, breaking chunks of cheese from the slab, chewing the yeasty, buttery biscuits as she watched him, tranquil, small and alluring.

"Thou art the strangest creature that ever I did see," she said. "What is thy name?"

"Morgan," he said around a mouthful of cheese and biscuits. He took a deep drink of water. "Shelter Morgan."

"Shelter? The name is comforting. Come, bring thy water jug and thy remnants of food. We must return to the temple."

"Temple?" Shelter shook his head. "You're very lovely, lady, but I'm not going wandering off anyplace with you."

"Thou trusteth me not?" she asked, a faint smile playing around the corners of her mouth.

"Not much. Do you have to talk that way?"

"To talk . . . of course, thou hast been taught to speak the new language." She nodded soberly. "I can speak that as well although it is strange to my ears. I have had to

38

practice for when we go forth into the pagan world." She got that out with a deal of effort.

Shelter had travelled with some Quakers once and her manner of speech reminded him of those stern, tight-laced people, but he had never seen a Quaker going around in a long white robe. He was seeing more and learning less these past two days than at anytime in his life.

"Who are you?" he asked. "What are you doing here?"

"I should ask first what thou art . . . what you are doing here, stranger. As for me, this is the citadel. Where else would a daughter of Kamolay wish to live?"

"Naturally," Shell said with a wry smile. "And what art thou called, daughter of Kamolay?"

"Freida." Her eyes turned down slightly and then lifted again, as open and innocent as ever. "Come, Shelter Morgan, we must go to the temple. You will follow me."

"Freida, I don't want to hurt your feelings, but just how in hell do I know what your intentions are? How do I know what I'm getting into?" At her curious look he explained, "How do I know I shall be safe?"

"Because I aver it," she said as if utterly surprised at Shelter's mistrust. "Besides, Shelter Morgan, what else will you do? Wait here with no food and no water, with no friends until you do wither?"

That made for a stronger argument. What indeed? He turned reluctantly and picked up the water jug by its narrow neck and nodded to Freida.

"Let's go. If you aver it to be safe refuge."

She smiled, not aware of the faint sarcasm in Shell's words. She turned and walked away, beckoning, and

Shelter found himself following, following the dark, beautiful woman toward the temple, the citadel, this place of refuge on a broad, empty mesa in the middle of an empty, savage desert.

4.

Moonlight silvered the cedar trees and glossed the grassy flats beyond. It danced in Freida's hair and made gossamer of the white robe she wore. Shelter followed, watching the lithe, easy movement of her body, the ingenuous swaying of her flaring hips, the straight line of her back.

He had to shake himself out of his reverie. There were others on this mesa not half so friendly. At least one.

A man with a bow and steel-tipped arrows who killed from concealment.

Even that was understandable in a way. Shelter had desecrated a grave, was found stealing buried treasure.

He could understand it all right; but he didn't like it one damned bit.

He walked beside Freida now, trying to probe a little.

"It was you the other night on the desert."

41

"Yes."

"It was you who bandaged my arm."

"Is it all right now?" she asked with concern.

"Yes. Why did you empty my pistol?"

"Oh, I had to do that."

"You had to?"

"Of course. Life is sacred, Shelter. You cannot have the means to take a life at your disposal."

"Well and good, Freida, But those Apaches damn sure had the means at their disposal and they meant to kill me."

"They would not harm you after seeing me," she said with a wave of her hand.

"Why not? How could you know?"

"They would not," she said, closing the subject.

They had come out of the woods and were heading in the direction of the tombstones. Shell slowed his pace, searching the moon shadows. Ambush? It was difficult to doubt this peaceful, small woman, but Shelter had only survived as long as he had by not being too trusting.

She was leading him now toward the very tombstone where the assassin had disappeared and Shell held up, gripping Freida's arm.

"All right. What is this?"

She turned to him, her face moonlit and lovely. Innocent, was she? Or only a great actress. "What do you mean? You are squeezing my arm. You must not give pain to anyone. It is against the way."

"I'll give a hell of a lot more pain if I don't start getting some straight answers," Shell said. "What's going on? Where are you leading me."

"To the temple, to our home."

"Not this way. Someone tried to kill me over there. A

man in a white robe. Wouldn't be anybody you might know, I don't suppose.''

"*I* know!" She gasped. "I know no one who would kill. I have told you we do not do violence. It is not the way of Kamolay.''

He looked intently at her, trying to read those dark eyes. He saw nothing there but surprise and gentleness.

"All right," he said, "you go first."

"Yes, I shall. How else would you find your way?'' she said logically. Could anyone be so guileless as she seemed? Could anyone raised in this world be so innocent of violence and hatred, of mistrust and deceit? She seemed to be of another world and Shelter, shaking his head, followed as she walked through the ranks of tall, bleak tombstones.

She walked directly to the stone behind which Shelter's attacker had hidden and Shell, still hanging back, still wary, watched as she walked to the massive slab of basalt and leaned against it.

It moved! The gigantic stone tilted toward Shell and swung up at the base. Somehow by pressing the exact spot on this mountainous gravestone she had managed to move it aside.

Incredulous, Shell walked to where Freida stood.

"It is not so difficult," she said, "it is perfectly balanced.''

In the darkness Shelter couldn't make out how the thing worked. Freida simply stood, hands clasped, looking at him. "We must go now," she said mildly.

"Go?" Then Shelter looked to where she gestured. Below the stone Freida had moved a narrow tunnel opened up. Crude steps had been carved into the ancient stone of the tunnel. From somewhere far below a dim light shone.

"Down there?" he asked.

"Of course. Come along now," she said, lifting her robe as she stepped into the shaft, Shelter gawking. "Please do hurry. The stone will return to its position. I should think a man standing where you are might be harmed."

More like crushed to damp powder, Shell decided, eyeing the rock again. He wasn't anxious to follow her, but as she had said earlier—what else was he going to do?

Shell turned and clambered down, his boots seeking the narrow, time-smoothed steps. Freida was already quite a way down. He could hear her urging him. What in hell am I getting into? he wondered.

Above him he heard a rasping creak and as he watched the huge monolith indeed began to tilt back into position, blotting out the moonlight and all of the world beyond the tunnel mouth.

Shell sighed and followed Freida down into the bowels of the mesa, scenting an unusual, indefinable smell like incense or burning cinnamon.

She had reached a narrow platform—a stony ledge cut into the wall of the cavern and she waited for Shell there. He stopped, caught his breath and looked downward where he could still see the dim glow of lanternlight, see three more stone ledges each with stone steps leading to them.

"This way," Freida said and he followed her to another flight of steps.

They must have gone down a hundred and fifty feet, passing an occasional torch hanging in iron brackets, before they came to a roomy subterranean alcove with a floor nearly as smooth as a manmade structure, lighted by rows of torches, In the walls niches had been cut and in these niches stood small effigies.

"The saints," Freida said, following Shell's gaze, answering his unspoken question.

She led off down the corridor and Shell asked, "Where are we going?"

"To the council chamber, of course."

"Of course." Naturally, where else but the council chamber. "Why?"

"That's where my father will be at this time of the day."

"Your father."

"I am Kamolay's daughter," she explained proudly, with a toss of her pert head.

"Ah. I hadn't realized that."

"You are the strangest creature I have known, Shelter Morgan. And the most comely."

"Comely?"

"Pleasing to my sexual self," she said, and Shell stumbled a little.

"Oh." He had a thought—"How long have you lived down here, Freida?"

"How long?" She stopped and looked up at him with warm, soft eyes. She began a smile and broke it off. "What do you mean? I have always been here."

"You were born here!"

She shrugged. "It is not in my memory. I just know that I have always been here. The council chamber is a little farther on," she said, moving out again.

Shell shrugged and followed her. This woman had been born here? Underground. Living out an entire life in this mesa? Not likely, Shell thought, but the way she had said it he almost believed it. Maybe—this thought came a

45

moment later—there was something wrong with this woman. Maybe she doesn't know the truth from a lie. There was something about her which was all wrong.

"Here." Freida smiled. They stood before a heavy oak door, one with no door handle, set into the solid gray granite around it. "It is the council chamber," she explained.

Or a trap.

Shell took a deep breath and closed his eyes momentarily. This was all getting stranger and stranger. What sort of people would live down here? What sort would carve the interior of this mountainous mesa away and make it their home? Raise their daughters here. Bury their dead with thousands in gold beside them. Walk the desert without shoes, apparently without weapons but bows and arrows.

The door creaked open and Shelter was taken in.

There was a long table running the length of the chamber. It was massively carved and had to be all of thirty feet long by ten wide. At intervals candles in intricate iron holders sat upon the table, and at the head of it, sitting with his hands cupping the arms of a tall, brass-studded chair sat the old man.

The old man. Shelter had seen him the other night out on the desert. He wore long white robes and a long white beard. His eyes gleamed in the candlelight. His face seemed utterly placid. Freida went to him, knelt down and kissed his hand.

"And who have you brought with you, Freida?" the old man asked in a voice richly resonant yet soft. His eyes, those unwavering, measuring eyes were on Shelter.

"This is Shelter Morgan, Father."

"The man from the desert. The man of guns." There

was no accusation in those words, only sorrow. Freida stood now, holding her father's hand.

"I am Kamolay, the Seventh Prophet. Please take a seat at my left hand."

Shelter did so, looking over the room as he pulled a chair away from the heavy table and sat. The council chamber seemed to have been a natural cavern, cut out of the solid stone by water or volcanic turbulence in the distant past. The ceiling was fifty feet or more above Shell's head. It was arched, irregular gray stone. The walls of the cavern had been chipped at until they were fairly smooth. They had been decorated with crudely made, symbolic wooden sculptures which Shell couldn't make head nor tail of.

"We had hoped, of course, that you would find your horse and ride on to the pagan lands," Kamolay was saying. "Why did you not?"

"The Apaches came back," Shell said.

"Indeed?" the old man stroked his white beard. "I would not have thought they would return after we visited them."

"Visited them?" Shelter asked in disbelief. This old man walking into a Chiricahua camp and holding a pleasant discussion with the Apaches?

"I should perhaps say we visited ourselves upon them. That we appeared to them, Mister Morgan."

Shell had noticed already that the old man didn't speak with the "thee and thou" his daughter had first used, which seemed odd if he had been the one to educate her. It suggested that Kamolay himself had been brought up out in that "pagan" world.

Still, looking at him, Shell saw no more deviousness, no more guile in those eyes than he was able to detect in

Freida's. He seemed a simple but strong man. Open yet reluctant to reveal himself to strangers. Mild, sincere.

"Just what are you people doing here?" Shell asked suddenly.

Kamolay looked deeply surprised. "Why—this is our home, Mister Morgan."

"This?" Shell gestured with an arm.

"Of course. It is our place away from the corruption of the pagan civilization beyond the desert."

"And the Apaches don't bother you?"

"Of course not . . . oh, Brother Thomas, come in."

Shelter glanced toward the doorway to see a man of middle years standing there. He was clean shaven, had slightly long, curling silver hair, a frank, open expression and a mild smile.

"I wondered if you needed anything, Father. I knew you had a guest. I wondered if he would like to be fed."

"Brother Thomas is our provisioner, Mister Morgan. He is in charge of all of our stores. Would you like to eat?"

Shell had a notion to say no, but his body objected strenuously. The cheese and dry biscuits hadn't done much for him.

"I wouldn't mind."

"I will see to it," Brother Thomas said, bowing away.

"Let me see," Kamolay went on, "I believe we were talking about our relationship with the Apaches. They are a superstitious lot, Mister Morgan. We have had to practice deceptions on them—regrettable, but necessary. They have seen us vanish in clouds of smoke, disappear into the ground . . ." he smiled almost with embarrassment. "That was necessary in the early days when we were seeking to establish ourselves in the citadel."

48

"Where did you come from?" Shell asked.

"Many places, sir," Kamolay said. "Here and there. All of the seekers, the miserable, the faithful."

Brother Thomas came in and, still smiling as if Shelter was his lifelong friend, he set a tray before him, a carved wooden trencher, and beside it a clay jug filled with that sweet water.

The trencher held raw, crooked carrots, cabbage in vinegar, turnips quartered and sprinkled with some red spice and piñon nuts.

"Our fare does not seem to please you," Kamolay said. Brother Thomas stood wringing his hands as if grief-stricken.

"I was imagining a T-bone and potatoes," Shell said in response.

"We would never eat beef, Mister Morgan. Brother Thomas' expressive hands fluttered about in shocked revulsion. "The cattle have to be murdered to produce beef. The very idea is against all we stand for, all we honor. The sacredness of life, the disavowal of any form of violence."

"Sure." Shell started gnawing on a carrot stick as Brother Thomas backed out the door. Freida sat across the table, watching him with glittering eyes. Kamolay stroked his beard and watched benevolently.

"You do not seem to accept what I say, Mister Morgan."

"I accept it. It seems that you've got some people among you who don't, however,"

"I do not understand you," Kamolay said.

"No." Shell leaned back, grimacing at the plate of raw vegetables. "I'll explain it to you. Someone from this citadel, someone who follows you, who wears your robes,

49

took a shot at me with a bow and arrow. A shot meant to kill me, Kamolay.''

Kamolay was smiling benignly, his eyes dancing with amusement.

"Something funny?" Shell asked.

"Your tale."

"It wasn't funny when it happened."

"But it is absurd! It cannot be. Surely your attacker must have been a pagan Apache."

"Wearing white robes?"

"You must have imagined that. How was the light?"

"Excuse me?"

"Was it daylight or night, dusk or dawn when this happened," Kamolay inquired.

"Sundown. The light was poor, but my eyes aren't that bad, Kamolay. It was a man in a white robe and he meant to kill me.''

"I cannot accept that. You may as well tell me the moon has fallen."

"I haven't been up tonight to check on that," Shell said dryly. "But this I can tell you, one of your people attacked me. He used a bow and arrow."

"A bow and arrow!" Kamolay was still smiling. His chest rose and fell as with soft laughter.

"Yes. A steel tipped arrow. I found it and examined it." Shell glanced at Freida. She was not amused. She wasn't even listening. She was staring at Morgan with deep, engrossed eyes, but her thoughts weren't on the story.

"We have no weapons at all, Mister Morgan." Kamolay's hands rose expressively. "We have no wish to kill. That is why we are here, why we have come together, why we are hidden away from the world and its violence.

To raise one's voice angrily in the citadel is the greatest criminal offense, but we have never even had a violation of that law. Our people are soft as doves' wings, it is the way, our way, and we follow it scrupulously.''

Except for one man, Shell thought.

"Perhaps there was a reason," Shell said out loud. "I stumbled onto a grave up there. Unintentional, it was, I was looking for water."

"One of the saints' graves," Kamolay said.

"I don't know about that."

"All of our people who die are saints, Mister Morgan. That is the term we use to refer to the dead."

"Then it was one of the saints," Shell agreed. "Anyway, as I say, I accidentally dug up one of them. Maybe it was an act of desecration, maybe you have a law that anyone disturbing a grave should be punished."

"Of course not." Kamolay smiled again. "How can the dead be disturbed? Anyway, we have no law which includes physical punishment. We are no longer pagans. Our only penalties are minor ones—a lesser portion at mealtime, a day's silence, and banishment as a last resort, but we have never had to banish anyone from among us . . ." Distantly a bell rang through the cavern. A great booming bell which seemed to shake the solid stone under Morgan's feet.

"Vespers," Kamolay said. "I must soon be going."

"There is the gold of course," Shelter said quietly.

"Sir?"

"The gold," Morgan repeated. "When I dug up the grave I found a pot full of gold."

"Yes?" Kamolay lifted an eyebrow curiously.

"Well, that might be reason enough to kill me, to prevent me from taking the gold."

51

"Why?"

"Because men like gold," Shelter said in exasperation. "They have been known to kill for it."

"In the pagan lands."

"Everywhere I've been," Shell said.

"But you have only lived in the pagan lands." Kamolay seemed to chuckle softly again. "Here what use is there for gold? We brought it with us in the days when we needed pagan money to buy pagan goods, before we had shut ourselves away from the death of the outside world. Now we have no use for it—or only an occasional use, I should say. In the beginning the gold was divided up, each man having an equal share. As none of us here have any need for gold, it is buried with us when we die."

"Why?"

"Sir?"

"Why bury it with the body? The saint has no use for it."

"No, sir. That precisely is the reason. He has no use for it. And we, looking down into the grave know that we will one day have no use for any of this world's possessions. Now," Kamolay said rising, "I must go to vespers. I hope we shall speak another time. For now you would probably like to wash and lie down. You and my daughter may take care of your sexual needs together if you like, and I will see you tomorrow, Mister Morgan. Goodnight."

The old man rose and Shelter stood as he did. There was one part in that little speech that flitted by before Shell could react to it. That part about taking Freida and bedding her. Shelter was looking at Freida, seeing her dark eyes sparkle, seeing the rise and fall of her full, firm breasts. The girl kissed her father's hand once again and

52

then Kamolay swept from the room, leaving them alone.

"Come, Shelter," Freida said. "I am sure a bath would cool you. I am sure you would like to lie down with me and comfort yourself with my body."

She took his hand, smiling, backing away as she led Morgan toward the door. He followed helplessly, hypnotized by the promise in those eyes, the silent magic of this strange and gentle woman.

5.

Shelter followed the girl through a long, winding stone corridor. They were passed at intervals by men in white robes, usually bearded, their hands tucked inside their sleeves, walking solemnly, quickly toward the distantly ringing bell.

"Freida."

Coming around the bend they had come face to face with a young man wearing a curly mop of blond hair and a hangdog expression.

"Good vespers, Brother Bartholomew."

"Good vespers, Freida." His eyes were climbing all over her. "You must hurry or you will be late for the last tolling."

"I cannot come with thee, Brother Bartholomew. See thee not that I am with a stranger? He needs to be attended."

"Yes." The young man bit his lip. "Good vespers to thee, stranger."

"Uh . . . good vespers," Shell replied.

Brother Bartholomew started to say something else, but he nodded instead and hurried on, glancing backward as he rounded the bend in the corridor.

"A friend?" Shelter asked.

"Brother Bartholomew and I give each other comfort," Freida said with a shrug. "Come along now."

Shelter followed, shaking his head. Gave each other comfort, did they? From that look lurking just beneath the mock serenity in Brother Bartholomew's eyes, Shell had the idea that Brother Bartholomew would like to give Shelter something a long way from comfort.

They passed a dozen men walking in a file, heads bowed, cowls raised, hands folded. No one spoke. "The men of misery," Freida whispered.

Shell looked back at the hooded men. He didn't ask—probably the answer wouldn't have made any sense either. The men of misery were gone and they had arrived at a heavy door facing onto the corridor. Shelter noticed this one had no handle, no lock also. He mentioned it to Freida.

"For what purpose would a door be locked?" she asked in astonished amusement. Shelter could only shrug. He was doing a lot of shrugging lately. He was going to wear out his shoulders.

He was in some sort of wonderland, no sense expecting anything to make sense, no point in asking questions. Freida closed the door behind them, immediately stepped out of her robe and walked across the small room. Shell's jaw fell.

She was astonishingly beautiful. That formless robe

had concealed a part of her, had hidden those ripe, bobbing breasts, the sleek thighs, the smooth sweep of her buttocks. Now she stood revealed, and she was as unselfconcious as a doe in her nakedness. Wild and beautiful and compelling.

She turned, smiling as she saw Shelter's lingering gaze.

"You see, I knew that you needed comfort. Come, let us bathe you. I will do it quickly so that we may immediately satisfy our sexual selves."

Shell had known some women. A lot of them. All sorts of women in all sorts of places, under odd circumstances, but he had never come across anything to beat this.

The woman was whistling as she bent low over a crudely made tub, her buttocks smooth and inviting thrust up toward Morgan who felt the blood begin to surge through his body, to pound at his temples.

"I shall procure the water. Do you take off your tight clothing and stand ready."

Ready. Hell, he was more than ready. He unbuttoned his ragged shirt and stepped from his torn jeans. Freida, walking to a small alcove in the back of the chamber, looked over her bare shoulder and smiled.

She was back in minutes, lugging two heavy wooden buckets filled with water. She looked him up and down, her smile lingering.

"My, you are in need of comfort, Shelter Morgan."

Understatement. Shell was hungry, mad with it, there must have been steam coming from his ears. She poured the water into the tub, bending over again to test it, again lifting that lovely ivory-white bottom toward him.

"You see, it is naturally warm."

"I'll bet."

"The water," Freida frowned although her eyes were smiling. "It does bubble up from a hot spring. It is a mineral water and is very healthy."

He simply stared until she told him, "Do you get into the tub now and I shall bring you more water. We have soap as well, a good yarrow soap as the Indians use, but scented with sage. It is a pleasing scent."

Shelter brushed past her, feeling the silk of her skin against his and he stepped into the tub, settling slowly.

Freida made a dozen trips back and forth from the alcove to the tub. Then looking down at him she said, "Shall I aid thee? If I rub your body it will cleanse and stimulate you, will it not?"

"It will stimulate me," Shell said, not sure that he needed or could take any more stimulation just then. She stood beside him, her legs wide spread, her pink-budded breasts full and ripe. She leaned forward and Shell lifted a hand, cupping her breast lightly. She hummed and rubbed his leg with both hands, scrubbing him with the yarrow soap which indeed had a fine scent.

But not as fine as the scent of Freida's young body, overripe, lush, flowing with the juices of a young woman. Shell reached up and grabbed her around the waist, pulling her into the tub. She sat on his lap, smiling as he kissed her breasts, let his hand run along the length of her thigh and gently search her cleft.

"Then you are through with your bath?" Freida asked, her hands around his neck, her breasts against him, her eyes sparkling.

"All through."

"Good. It is well. My sexual needs are burgeoning," Freida said.

They weren't burgeoning half as much as Shelter's, as

she saw and noted as they stepped from the tub. "Perhaps we should attend to this quickly," she suggested.

"Perhaps we should." Shell looked around. Where?"

"Here, come with me. Here is my bed. Will it do? I know so little of the strangers' ways."

It was a thin little mattress on the stone floor of the cavern. Stuffed with pine needles and leaves, it was a poor place for sleeping. It was suitable for this—anything would have been: a bed of nails, a cactus patch.

"Come lie down and do enter me," Freida said and she lay back, holding Shell's hand as she lifted her knees and spread her legs, touching herself, reaching with anxious fingers for Shelter. "Come now. Do enter me," she said, and since Shell's mama had taught him never to deny a woman's request, he lay down with her, fitting himself between those lovely uplifted legs, feeling her groping fingers position him and urge him to enter.

He obliged.

She shuddered as he touched home. Her hands went to his shoulders and slid down his spine, finding his buttocks. She clenched him tightly, lifting him with her pelvis, pulling him down with her hands as her breathing quickened and her body trembled.

She hummed softly for a time as Shelter rode her. His lips found her breasts. His tongue toyed with her taut pink nipples and still she hummed, saying softly:

"I am finding sexual satisfaction now. Are you, Mister Morgan? Oh! I am finding sexual satisfaction, my goodness! It is all feeling good. I am starting to come apart— oh my gosh, I am finding it all over the place!"

And Shell battered against her, his hand beneath her buttocks, lifting her as he drove it home time and again as Freida's mouth went slack and her murmuring became indistinct gurgling deep in her throat.

"I have never . . . found sexual satisfaction like this before!" Then she screamed and Shell settled into the hilt as she writhed and tossed beneath him, her flesh growing glossy with beads of perspiration, as she bit at his nose and throat with her small, even, quite sharp teeth.

She reached up, clenched his hair in both hands screamed again and then came completely undone, twisting beneath him like a fish on a hook, moaning softly in a steady cadence as Shelter reached an answering, hard climax.

They lay together in the cavern, listening to the thumping of their hearts, to their slowing breathing. Shell stroked her body, fondled her lovely, lush breasts, teased her ear with his lips and tongue.

After a minute she opened her eyes wide and looked at him with astonishment. She started to rise.

"What is it?" Shelter asked from out of his lethargy.

"Why, nothing. It was very fine. I have been sexually satisfied and I know that you have. Now I must go to my other duties. I feel a wonderful glow and I know I shall perform my tasks merrily."

With that she was out from under him, padding across the room to where her robe had fallen. She slipped it over her head and smiled at him.

"Do you sleep, Mister Shelter Morgan. I understand that a man might feel this is a good time for that relaxation." Then she was gone.

The big door swung to and Shelter was left alone in the cavern room, his mind cluttered with a hundred questions, his body very, very relaxed.

Still he did not sleep. He got out of the bed, slipped into his clothes and walked to the door. Opening it a crack

59

he peered out, seeing no one.

He eased out into the corridor, looking either way. No one was around.

There was something wacky about this set-up, but Morgan couldn't figure what it was. A colony of white robed fanatics living underground out here. People who hated violence yet had tried to kill him. People who were as casual about sex as any Shelter had even heard of. People who buried gold money with their dead.

And just where in hell had that gold come from? How many people lived down here? Hundreds. Multiplied by five thousand dollars—the amount the dead "saint" had earned as his share. Share of what?

Shell walked back toward the entrance to the cavern, climbing the narrow stone steps in the near darkness. He wanted to have a look at that entranceway. When he decided it was time to go, he wanted to make sure he *could* leave.

He found his way back easily, passing no one. They were all presumably at vespers—doing whatever white-robed fanatics did at such times.

He found the base of the monolith and pressed his hands against it, finding it as unyielding as the solid stone wall beside him. He experimented, trying various spots, searching for hidden levers, for any kind of keystone. There was nothing.

When he finally gave it up he was sweaty and utterly frustrated. He wasn't going to get out of this place unless and until they wanted him to leave, and for all of their mildness, their assumed friendliness, Shelter didn't like it a bit.

He walked back down the stairs, running a few more questions through his mind. One, where in hell were they growing those vegetables? He had seen nothing like a garden on top of the mesa. They needed sunlight to grow that stuff, however. Two, where did they get the cloth, the metal, the various small but, he assumed, store-bought articles they had?

There was oxygen in this cave. He was breathing well enough, the torches on the wall burned brightly. There had to be another way out and they had to use it from time to time to go somewhere—Delgado?—to purchase the things they could not make.

He set off to find it.

He passed the door to Freida's room, passed the council chamber and continued on. From far below—or above, he couldn't tell—came the murmuring of hundreds of voices. That would be the vespers, he assumed.

They were still busy then. He had a little more time to poke around.

Now he began to pass more tunnels, some crudely cut, unlighted, leading off in a dozen different directions. Leading where?

Shell turned right, ducked low and entered a chamber which seemed larger than the rest. He walked on a way, feeling the moisture underfoot. Water seeping in from somewhere.

The tunnel opened up quickly, growing high and wide. A cold draft whistled up the passageway as Shelter emerged into a section some fifty feet wide, half that high with an arched ceiling. There were no torches here, but Shelter could see tolerably well.

With good reason. The moon was shining directly into the open mouth of the tunnel. Stars blinked brightly in the dark sky. Shelter was looking out on the broad eastern desert from a height of three hundred feet, possibly more.

He moved nearer to the edge and saw immediately that there was no way down here. The wall of the precipice, actually the side of the mesa, fell away at a sharp angle. No man could climb that and he had no intention of trying.

The footsteps behind him brought Shell's head around sharply. As he turned the arrow *thwanged* from the bow string.

The arrowhead clipped a button from the front of Shelter's shirt. Had he not been turning it would have struck him dead square in the middle of the back.

He charged up the dark cavern tunnel, hearing frantic receding footsteps ahead of him. Then he heard them no more.

Walking cautiously forward, his knife in hand, Shell found a small branch tunnel he had not seen on the way in. He ducked his head and entered. It was as black as sin, deathly still.

He paused, leaning his head near to the stone wall. He couldn't detect a whisper of sound. Inching forward Shell found another tunnel mouth on his right, and a few steps farther on, one on his left.

The assassin, whoever he was, was gone.

But assassin is what he was. In this citadel of peace and love there was someone who was not exactly peaceful or loving.

The same one as the one who had tried to kill him up above? Probably, although perhaps Shelter had given someone else the idea by talking about the first incident. Like who? Kamolay? Or Brother Bartholomew, the young man who usually gave Freida her sexual comfort?

Maybe it was the whole bunch of them. Maybe they were covering up something they didn't want an interloper stumbling onto.

The speculation was endless. One thing was certain—there was someone in this cavern who had tried to kill Shelter Morgan. Someone who would keep on trying until he got it right.

6.

There wasn't much left of Shelter's clothing. In the morning Freida appeared with a robe for him to wear. "Come along, there is much to do," she said cheerfully, but with no hint of the sexuality of the night before.

Shell stepped naked from her bed and reached for his gunbelt. The Colt was empty, but the bowie was hanging from the same belt. He slung it around his naked hips to Freida's unconcealed amusement, and to her disgust, he thought, then slipped the robe over his head.

"Whatever do you want with those ugly trophies of the pagan world?" Freida asked. "Are they talismans for you?"

"Talismans for half the world, Freida," Shelter said. He added quietly, "My half."

He found that he could split the seam of the robe and have access to the bowie and he did that as Freida watched, her bright eyes wondering at this stranger.

"Why, nothing can hurt you here! How frightened you must be inside to feel the need for steel in your hands. You must try to find the inner peace which we all share in the citadel."

Sure. The inner peace which prompts folks to go around trying to put an arrow through someone's heart. These people had their own talismans.

After they had eaten—raw vegetables again—Freida stood and held out her hand to Shell.

"Now we must show you around the citadel a little. We will try to find you a job you will be comfortable with."

Shelter rose, his eyes narrowing. Freida was smiling but Morgan didn't reveal even a hint of amusement.

"I don't want a job, Freida."

"But you must work. Everyone who breaks bread must work. It takes work to produce food, work to earn it."

"Fine. I'm all in favor of that. I'm a great believer in working for your keep, but not me, not here." Shelter looked into those huge unblinking eyes and said, "What I want to do, Freida is get out of here. I want a horse and some water."

"But . . . ." she stammered and looked down, her fingers twisting together. "Aren't you happy with me? Didn't I satisfy your sexual needs."

"Stop it with that. There's more to my life than walking around in long robes, eating raw vegetables and being sexually satisfied even if you are a delightful woman."

"But you don't understand—"

"You cannot leave." The voice came from the doorway and Shelter turned that way. Kamolay stood there, his white beard flowing across his chest, his eyes fixed on

65

Morgan.

"And why not, Kamolay?"

"Something might happen to you, Mister Morgan. How can you cross the desert alone?"

What was Kamolay telling him? "Am I a prisoner?"

"A prisoner! Such a word. Of course not. We only fear for your safety if you should go out there alone."

Shelter was starting to fear for his safety if he didn't leave the citadel. It was impossible to read Kamolay's expression. He was wreathed in benevolence, his eyes friendly, open, warm. Yet Morgan was sure there was something else lingering in those eyes.

"I do not understand," Kamolay said slowly. "I offer you paradise and you wish to leave, why?"

"There's things I have to do out there."

"Terrible things. I see it in your eyes, Mister Morgan."

"Maybe."

"You destroy yourself with these obsessions, you drown your own spirit in dark perfidy."

"Have you got a horse I can borrow?"

"No."

"Will you give me water?"

"I do not think you are well enough to leave. Your arm . . ."

"Damn my arm, Kamolay! I want to get the hell out of here."

"I see," he said softly. "And go where?"

"Into Delgado."

"All right," he sighed. "It cannot be today. But from time to time we too must visit the pagan world; there are items our craftsmen are not skilled enough to manufacture which we purchase there. When Brother Thomas

66

next travels to Delgado, you may travel with him.''

Freida looked suddenly lost. Small and betrayed. ''I have to go,'' he said to her. ''When is your storekeeper going into Delgado next?''

''I will ask him and advise you. You will have time to regain your strength. Time perhaps to change your mind. Look around, Mister Morgan, see how we live, what sort of peace we have attained. Then ask yourself if you really must go out into the pagan world and do violence.''

With that Kamolay was gone, leaving Shelter to muse. Was he really going to let Morgan out of here? Or was Kamolay behind the attempts on his life? Maybe Kamolay was frightened silly that the outside world would find out about his citadel. After all, having taken precautions like this, it was obvious that concealment of the sect was of prime importance to the old man. Shelter could do nothing but remain alert and wait for his chance.

''Come now,'' a subdued Freida said, ''We shall visit the different areas of the citadel. Perhaps,'' she said, brightening, ''once you have seen all we have to offer, you will change your mind about leaving us.''

''Perhaps,'' Shell said tonelessly.

Freida took his arm and led him to the door. They had to wait a moment for the twelve hooded men who walked slowly past. The men of misery, Freida had termed them—whatever the hell that meant. It was impossible to make out the faces of the cowled men. They walked mechanically past, hands thrust into the sleeves of their robes, heads bowed, silent and ghostly.

''Come along,'' Freida said. She had recovered her good spirits, and she bounced along beside Shelter, holding his arm as they descended a long passageway and came upon a wide tunnel which was some sort of main thoroughfare. Here robed men and women, some with baskets over their arms as if they had been shopping, strolled along, all with that same innocent, nearly blank expression.

"This way." Freida made two turns and Shelter followed along, trying to remember every twist and turn of these tunnels. The place was a virtual maze and he soon lost count of how many rights, how many lefts they had made.

Brother Bartholomew appeared suddenly from around a bend in the tunnel and he blocked their way.

"Freida."

"Brother Bartholomew," she said in response. The young man looked at Shelter and there was a definite lack of hospitality in his eyes.

"Then the stranger will stay," he said flatly. Shelter wasn't getting any peace and love vibrations from Brother Bartholomew. He wiped back his mop of curly blond hair and looked at the floor.

"It has not yet been decided," Freida said and Shelter didn't contradict her.

"I see," Brother Bartholomew said, nodding his head slowly. "If that is how it must be."

Then without another word he brushed past them and was gone.

"Whatever can be troubling Brother Bartholomew?" Freida asked innocently and Shelter had to grin.

"You don't know?" At her negative shake of the head, he explained, "He doesn't want me sharing your sexual satisfaction."

"Oh, that is impossible! That cannot be. It is against the law to be possessive or selfish in these matters."

"Against the law," Shell repeated. It might be against

the law; but that was what was going on, and anyone outside of a girl who had spent her entire life underground with a bunch of robed zombies would have known it immediately. He said, "Lead on, Princess, let's see what the citadel has to offer a pagan."

They walked down another, much wider tunnel and found themselves on a wide ledge much like the one Shelter had seen the night before. This one, however, was cultivated. Soil brought up from who knew where had been spread across the ledge to a depth of three feet or so and a vegetable patch of several acres had been formed.

The morning sun beamed down onto the flourishing garden and white robed figures—men and women in about equal proportion—moved along the rows, chanting as they planted and hoed.

"You see!" Freida said cheerfully. "Everyone is happy. Everyone is working to bring forth food for the chosen ones."

"Uh-huh."

"But you do not wish to be a gardener."

"Not much."

Freida, temporarily crestfallen, brightened again. "Then come along, we have other occupations."

"How about showing me the stables, Freida."

"The stables?" she asked innocently.

"Yes." Shell nodded at the pile of horse manure which was being carried in buckets to the garden. They had horses somewhere and plenty of them.

"Let me show you the candlemaker's shop or the library."

"Freida." He took her arm. "I would like to see the stables."

"I cannot, Mister Morgan. My father has told me I

should not.''

"And so you won't."

"I cannot do what my father wishes me not to do."

"No, I guess you couldn't." Shell sighed. "All right, show me the candlemakers' shop."

She did. In a small alcove withered little men poured tallow into molds, glancing up with blank eyes at Shell and Freida only briefly. From there they went to the library where three men sat at a bench binding ancient books. There were volumes lining three crudely fashioned bookcases. The next stop was one which interested Shell a lot more.

Turning down still another torchlit corridor—were there an endless number of these damned things?—they came to the storeroom.

There was no door, no obstacle to entering. Of course no one in the citadel would ever think of stealing anything, so there wasn't much point in locking up the communal property, Shell supposed.

They found Brother Thomas and a helper squatting near a pile of bricks, counting them out. Shell noted the bricks, noted that he had not seen any bricks anywhere in this cavern.

"Good day to thee, Freida," Brother Thomas said standing. "And a good day to thee, stranger Morgan."

Shell nodded, Freida gave him a "good day" in return. "I have brought the stranger to examine the store room. One day he shall have to take a job and perhaps he would like to work here."

"That would be pleasant," Brother Thomas said, and Shell almost believed the silver-haired man meant it. He beamed with pleasure as Shell and Freida walked through his storeroom which was made up of four different, interconnected caves.

Shell looked over the assortment of goods carefully. Most of it was flour and salt, hides and bolts of linen cloth like the robes were made of. He had candle holders, some of those wrought iron brackets used for torches, mattresses, and hand tools.

"Brother!" Thomas's assistant called to him from the outer chamber and the store keeper said:

"Just a moment, please, Freida, stranger Morgan. I must see what he wishes."

With that Brother Thomas picked up his robes and went out, and Shelter couldn't have been more pleased with the timing. He had seen something he wanted badly. A small green box pushed to the back of a shelf. The printing on the box read: Remington Small Arms Company. Caliber .44-40.

A box of cartridges, tempting and close. Shell snatched the box from the shelf as Freida watched him in disbelief.

"What is that? Why are you taking it?"

"Now then—" Brother Thomas had returned before Shelter could answer. Freida stood gaping at him. Brother Thomas rubbed his hands together. "Is there anything else I can show you?"

"No. We've seen enough."

"Maybe you will come back and work for me, stranger Morgan."

"Maybe." Shell was watching Brother Thomas and Freida closely. Several times she opened her mouth as if she were going to say something, but nothing ever came out. She just stood there looking shocked and disappointed.

Brother Thomas said nothing else either, but just for a moment it seemed to Shell that his placid gray eyes flickered to the shelf where the cartridges had been. That might have been guilt interpreting the casual glance, however. With his hands stuffed into his long, concealing sleeves in imitation of the rest of these robed moles, Shell was able to walk out of the storeroom, the box of cartridges firmly in hand. He only hoped they weren't twenty years old.

He didn't wait long. After they had rounded the first bend, Shell tore the other seam in his robe, whipped out his Colt and opened the box of bullets.

He examined one, found it bright and new, and thumbed five cartridges rapidly into the cylinder of his Colt, holstering it again quickly before someone could come around the bend in the tunnel.

Freida was staring at him, aghast. Shell winked.

"You . . . you stole those."

"Yes. But then there's no one else who will ever have a use for them, is there, Freida? I mean, no one else has any weapons but me, isn't that so?"

"You could have asked. Brother Thomas would have given them to you perhaps."

"Perhaps wasn't good enough, Freida."

"The longer I know you, Shelter Morgan, the more I think you are a terrible man!" She glared at him, lip thrust out.

"I think it's against the 'law' to become angry, Freida," Shell said with a grin.

"Oh! You are terrible and wicked."

"But sexually satisfying," Shelter said with another grin. "Come on, show me the rest of the citadel, I'm feeling better about things now."

"Now that you can kill again."

"Show me," he repeated and she stomped off, Shell

72

following, still grinning.

They continued to travel downward into the heart of the mesa, Freida mechanically showing Morgan the various workshops and the people—all blank-eyed, seemingly dull-witted, inevitably robed—working at their trades.

"Which way out now?" Shell asked suddenly.

"I cannot tell you that."

"Because of your father?"

"Yes. He has not yet given his blessing on your departure."

"Freida, I don't really give a damn about his blessing. I want to know which way is out. I'd like you to show me that, and I'd like to be shown where the horses are kept."

"I do not . . ."

"Lying is against the law," he said as she stammered.

"I was not going to lie," she said hotly.

"No." They had come to another tunnel opening on the side of the mesa. Shell looked out and saw they were still a hundred feet up. Below the desert, that damnable thing, stretched out for a hundred miles, looking free and tantalizing after the long day Shell had spent in this citadel, this hole in the ground where madmen did—whatever they did. Made candles, planted lousy, crooked carrots, satisfied sexual appetites.

There was a way out of here, had to be. Brother Thomas, the storekeeper, went into Delgado occasionally. He must have horses and a wagon. He sure as hell didn't walk across that desert and tote his supplies back in a gunny sack.

"Why does your father want to keep me here?" Shell asked.

"He does not. You were brought here to be helped,

stranger Morgan. Do you not recall that you were hungry and we gave you food, you were thirsty and we gave you drink . . .''

"Yes. I recall it all. I appreciated it. But now I want out. This is a cozy prison, I suppose, if a man has to be in prison, but I've been in prison before and I didn't like it then. I don't like it now. If I could I'd stick a gun to someone's head and force them to show me the way out. Somehow I don't think it would work with this pack of zombies.''

She stood gaping at his "wickedness.''

His voice softened and he took her hand. "Let's sit down.''

They walked to the rim of the ledge and sat, their feet dangling into space, the dry breeze off the desert wafting past them.

"There's a whole world out there, Freida.'' Shelter gestured largely.

"It is desert.''

"It's not all desert. Beyond this there are rivers and trees, mountains, pretty little places.''

"It is pagan beyond the desert,'' she said, toying with the fabric of her robe.

"You're right there. It's pagan and it's violent and it's cruel. But not all of it, not always. There are good people out there too, good people interested in many things. Things you've never heard of.''

"I've read books,'' she said defensively.

"This place,'' Shell nodded, "it's a place for hiding away from reality, Freida.''

"From evil.''

"And from the good. You're all cripples here, Freida, do you realize that? Small, cramped people with small cramped ideas."

"No." Her response was quick, certain and final.

"What started all of this?" Shelter asked after a minute. He was looking across the desert toward the distant, chocolate colored hills, watching a dust devil snatch up a funnel of red dust; carry it twisting, leaping across the desert and deposit it as the dust devil quickly born, as quickly expired.

"I don't know what you mean," Freida said.

"I'm asking why your father came here. What happened out there?" he nodded toward the "pagan" lands. "Where did the money come from? All that gold which Kamolay has, so much that it's buried with the dead."

"That was the gift of Cassius Dormer," Freida said.

"Who?"

"Cassius Dormer who was the Benefactor. He was a troubled man, a sinner, elderly and ill. He is known as the Benefactor. My father went to him and told him of his vision. He told the Benefactor that he wished to lead his people into the desert to free their troubled spirits of the burden of that world."

"And Cassius Dormer forked over."

"Pardon me?" She tilted her head, her expression puzzled.

"Never mind. How did your father know about this mesa? Or did he know before he found it? He must have. He couldn't just have traipsed across the desert aimlessly."

"My father, in his first life, his sinful life, was a prospector. He knew of this mesa from his explorations."

"A prospector. He hit it with Dormer, didn't he?"

"Again I do not understand you, stranger Morgan." Freida looked off into the distances. "If you think my father cares about gold then why do you think he remains here? Why do you believe he buries the shares of the saints? No, Mister Morgan, my father cares nothing for pagan riches.''

"What about these 'men of misery'? Who are they? They're the only ones I see wearing hoods. What's special about them?''

"I cannot say. My father has never told me.'' She paused. "I am sure they are special men, very burdened by sadness, great sinners, perhaps or those who have suffered greatly.''

"All right. Stand up then. Here, give me a hand. I want to look around a little more.''

"There is nothing more to see, stranger Morgan.''

"The hell there isn't, Freida. Up to now I've been looking at what your father wanted me to see. Now I'm going to look at what he doesn't want me to find.''

7.

It was a guessing game with no solution. Morgan guided Freida along the long passages, moving deeper and deeper into the heart of the mesa, feeling that if a horse and wagon were ever taken out of the citadel they must exit near the floor of the desert. Certainly no team could be taken out the entrance Shell had used.

He asked Freida which way to go, but her lips were sealed. He could guess nothing from her expression either as they wandered through the endless, winding corridors.

Suddenly there it was.

They had come around a sharp, downward tending bend in the tunnel to find a solid wall. But the wall was not of native stone. Whatever was behind this had been bricked in. Bricks ran from ceiling to floor, chipped to fit the natural contours of the cave, solidly mortared, and

Shell decided after testing the wall, reinforced.

"What's behind this?" he demanded. Freida shook he head. "What?" She shook her head more furiously an Shelter, kicking the wall in frustration turned away, fol lowing a new corridor which angled downward still mor steeply.

"I do not like this. You are wicked. We should not b here."

The end of that tunnel dead-ended fifty yards on. Shel sighed, looking around. There were tunnels branchin every which way. In fact, he decided, it was a wonder th ancient mesa hadn't just collapsed. Honeycombed b caverns, it had been chipped away at by the Kamolay sec year after year. What had originally been volcanic c water-cut passages were widened and lengthened b man. Remembering the mass of earth and stone abov him was enough to give Shell the shudders.

"Where are the horses, Freida? You know I'll fin them eventually. Do you want to wander up and dow these corridors with me all day . . . ?" he fell silen Someone was approaching.

Shell stood silently at the end of the tunnel, Freida be hind him. But there was no threat. It was only two me with a huge wheelbarrow loaded with torches and a can c what had to be coal oil.

They took down the flaming torch, extinguished it an placed a new torch in the wall bracket. A necessary job but Morgan shook his head, thinking of these men war dering these caverns endlessly, keeping the lamps lit.

"All right, come on," Shelter said.

"Where?"

"To look for the horses."

"You'll never find them."

"Then I'll never quit looking," and watching those steady blue eyes of Shelter Morgan, Freida knew that he wouldn't. They would wander up and down the corridors until he finally found them.

"All right," she said with a heavy sigh and a tiny shake of her pretty head, "I'll show you where they are—if you promise me something."

"What's that?"

"Promise me that you won't take a horse. Not now, not today. Not until you've spoken to father again and asked him."

"All right," Shelter said a little reluctantly. He would like to have found the horses, straddled the best animal he could find and gotten the hell out of this stone madhouse, but he knew the search might be endless in this vast honeycomb. "I'll promise you that."

"You mean it? You must mean it." She searched his eyes anxiously.

"I promise, Freida," he said with a smile. He placed his hands on her shoulders and kissed her forehead.

"I do not want sexual satisfaction now."

"That's not what I held you for."

"Why else? That is the only time anyone touches me," she said and there was something pathetic in her words. Shell let his hands fall away.

"Let's get going," he said gruffly, watching as the small beautiful, lost woman slipped past him and glided quietly down the corridor.

Torchlight flickered on the walls, the floors, the ceiling. In between the torches there were deep pools of blackness. Freida flitted along the corridors, turning left and then right, disappearing in the deep shadows between the torches to reemerge eerily farther on. Shell stuck

79

close to her, not wanting to get lost in this endless place.

They were getting near now. They had continued to descend and Shelter's nostrils picked up the stable smells of horses, hay, manure.

Freida, her face drawn, looked back across her shoulder. She halted, lifting an arm.

"I am forbidden to go. Do not forget your promise."

"No." He walked past her, ducking low to clear a drop in the ceiling, rounded a right-hand bend and then he saw it.

He heard someone moving around, speaking in a low voice, saw a lanternlit alcove as big as any he had yet seen, saw a dozen horses standing in clean, neat stalls. One big bay was looking at him, ears pricked curiously.

There was a harness rack, several saddles sitting on saw horses, and a great wooden door which had to lead outside, onto the desert.

Shell saw a long shadow, heard the voice coming nearer, and he quickly retreated.

Freida was waiting, looking beaten and worried. "You came back!"

"I made you a promise."

"Yes, but I thought a wicked man like you . . ."

"Sure. Let's get out of here, Freida. I want to go back and talk to your father."

"You want to ask him for a horse again."

"That's right. I promised you I would ask him."

"If he refuses?"

"I'm going anyway."

"You would disobey the Kamolay after he has saved you from the Indians?" The shock in her voice was obvious.

"I would. I will. You people have been generous—

most of you—but I don't intend living the rest of my life underground. Bad as it is in those pagan lands, by God, I at least can feel the sun on my face, smell the earth around me, eat a steak, by God!''

Freida fell silent. She was no doubt dwelling on his wickedness again. Shelter touched her elbow.

"Let me take the lead, Freida. I want to see if I can find my way back to your room."

"You mean you want to learn your way to the stables so that you can steal a horse."

"If it's necessary, yes."

She shook her head with great sadness and let Shelter take the lead. Twice he made the wrong turn and Freida had to correct him; but imprinting each turn on his memory as he went, he felt certain he could find his way the next time. And the next time if he had his way, would be soon.

The hell with their robes, the hell with their arrows, the hell with their carrots! He was going. This wicked pagan was getting the hell out of this sterile sanctuary.

There was a man waiting for him in Delgado, and he didn't want to disappoint him. A man named Horatio Dabb, or Charles Dantworth. He had shed his old name, that murderer's name, that coward's name.

He could alter his name, but he couldn't alter the fact that he had lain in ambush for his own men, killing them for war booty, leaving others he had never seen to die over that long, bitter winter.

Shell grinned—he was before the council chamber. He had found his way back, not easily, but he had found his way.

"Will you speak to him now?"

"In a minute."

81

Shelter returned to his shared room and, casting the robe aside, he stepped into his torn jeans, his ragged shirt. Then he belted his Colt on again. He found his Winchester in the corner, loaded it to its full seventeen-shot capacity, dumped the rest of the cartridges from the green box into his shirt pockets and he was ready.

"Don't have a canteen, do you?"

"A what?" Freida asked. She was watching him with distress, her eyes large and unhappy, her mouth drooping.

"Never mind. Do you mind if I take this water jug?"

"Thou art asking now?" she said dryly.

"Back to 'thou', is it?" Shelter picked up the water jug, finding it nearly full.

"I only spoke in the new way for thy sake. Now why need I practice it, stranger Morgan?"

"Freida—do you want to come with me?"

"Go with thee!" her mouth dropped open and she slowly shook her head. "Art thou mad? Leave citadel, leave Kamolay?"

"Yes."

"It cannot be."

"All right. Listen, you said once that you were learning the 'new speech' against the day you would have to go out again into the pagan world. What did you mean? When do you have to go out? Why would you?"

"I know not."

"All right." Shell smiled but she didn't answer his smile. He stepped nearer to her and stroked her long dark hair.

"Why art thou touching me?"

"Because I like you, Freida. Do you understand that? I think you're remarkable at sexual satisfaction, but I also happen to like you.''

"I do not understand," she said sadly, and the awful part was that Shelter believed her. They didn't show a lot of emotion in the citadel. Maybe nobody had ever told her before, "I like you."

"So long, Freida. I'm going now. You've been kind. Thank you."

She didn't answer. She turned numbly and watched as he went out the doorway and turned toward the council room and Kamolay.

The old man was seated at the head of the table, eyes half shut as Shelter entered. He greeted Shell quietly: "Stranger Morgan, I see you are troubled."

"I am troubled, Kamolay. I'm troubled by this citadel. I'm leaving. I want a horse."

He placed the water jug and his rifle on the long table. Kamolay nodded slowly, heavily.

"I knew that you were wrong for this place when I first saw you. I knew that you would not stay, would not adopt our tranquil ways, would not accept work, peace, simple food."

"You were right. I'm going and I'm going now."

"Then it is the end for us."

"What do you mean?"

Shell stepped nearer. The old man had his chin on his chest. With his full white beard it looked like his head was floating on a cottony sea.

"I mean, stranger Morgan, that I must let you leave. How can we stop you? And once you have gone you will tell others about the citadel and they will return with more guns and they will destroy all that we have built. Destroy a civilization, Morgan, do you understand that?"

"Yes. Listen, Kamolay, this might not mean anything

to you, but I give you my word that I won't say anything about this mesa. I don't want to hurt you or your people, I simply want to get back into my world."

"I can almost believe you, stranger Morgan," Kamolay said, wiping his hand back across his long white hair. "In fact I have no choice but to believe you." He smiled wanly. "So be it. If your oath is not true, then we shall leave. I have always known we would one day be discovered, always known that we would one day have to return to the pagan world—I only hoped that it would not be so soon."

"It need not be for a long time, Kamolay. No matter what you might think of me, I assure you—my word means something."

"Yes," Kamolay looked at Morgan closely, studying the tall man with the blue eyes, the firm jaw, the flat cheeks. "I believe it does," the old man said, and Shelter almost believed the old man was sincere.

There you go again, Shell, he said to himself. Mistrustful bastard, aren't you? Yeah, he answered, but a living one. He had more faith in his Colt than in Kamolay's word, but still he bid the old one farewell and assured him again that he wouldn't reveal anything about the citadel.

Wearily Kamolay smiled and wished Morgan well in the pagan lands.

Shell nearly bumped into Brother Bartholomew as he stepped into the corridor.

"Get an earful, Bartholomew?" Shell asked.

"What . . . ?" Bartholomew stammered, his face going crimson. His youthful eyes glittered.

"Know something, son? You're too excitable for this life. Rest easy—I'm leaving and you've got Freida back."

"Soiled," he managed to croak. He said it again. "Soiled," and he broke into a run, dodging up the corridor, arms outflung.

Shell, grinning, turned away. "I hardly used it," he muttered.

He worked his way down through the immense cavern cautiously, his eyes searching the shadows, hand clenching the Winchester. He met no one until he found the silver-haired Brother Thomas at the stable far below ground.

"You have come for a horse," Thomas said.

Shell blinked with surprise. "How did you know that, Thomas?"

"We have our methods of communication," the mild man said with a shrug. "But I knew you would be leaving anyway. A man like you cannot fit into our peaceful society. I saw this in your eyes when we first met."

"You were right," Shell told the provisioner. "I don't know how I can return this horse to you."

"Please," Brother Thomas answered, "do not attempt it. It would only risk our discovery. Have you money to buy another horse?"

"No," Morgan admitted.

"Then do keep this one. It is easy for us to obtain more." Brother Thomas took Shell's arm. "Come. Show me the animal you would like, and it will be yours."

The small, gray-eyed man patiently let Shelter examine every horse in the stable and Morgan finally chose a leggy roan with three white stockings.

"Over here then are the saddles and bridles—seldom used, obviously. Here is a saddle blanket. And I do have somewhere a water skin which will be easier for you than a jug."

Thomas waited, hands folded, until Shell was finished saddling the roan which took the bit reluctantly. Then Thomas smiled and said, "I wish you well whatever you are doing. We have tried to be giving. Peace go with you. Do not return, Stranger Morgan—this is the message Kamolay has asked me to give you. Go in peace, but do not look back."

Having said that Thomas summoned two burly men who worked in the stable. They went to the massive oaken gate and swung it open.

Brilliant white sunlight flooded the dark stable. Shelter winced. The heat and light swept over him. He heeled the horse forward before anyone could say another word and in seconds he was out onto the broad, empty, barren, beautiful desert.

He halted the roan and looked back to see the gates swinging shut. The gates were beautifully camouflaged, plastered over with reddish mud which duplicated the mesa wall, screened by head high sagebrush. When the gates were fully closed Morgan could see not a trace of the opening, and the world of the citadel, the strange underground world peopled with white robed monkish men, strange innocent, unloved girls, seemed to fade into unreality. It might have all been a dream, but the horse beneath him wasn't imaginary, nor was the warm memory of a night of contentment spent with Freida with the gentle eyes.

"Come on, horse," Shelter said. "We've got a lot of desert to cover." And somewhere out there the Chiricahua Apache still lurked. Somewhere ahead lived the man who must die, Horatio Dabb. Shelter pushed the citadel out of his mind. His reality now was the vengeance trail and the long miles of red desert. He lifted the roan into a ground-devouring canter, eyes raised to the horizon, anxious for his first glimpse of Delgado.

8.

Delgado was a low scab on the flat desert. Nine weather faded frame buildings standing in a dreary row along a main street, facing each other with blank faces and dead eyes, a dozen adobe houses built back along a dry wash where cottonwoods grew in profusion. A bank which looked like a doll house, a general store, once green, with the paint now peeling, and three saloons provided all of the town's apparent assets.

Shelter walked the roan down the main street of Delgado as sunset flooded the western skies with a fantastic display of crimson and gold. The red earth streets of Delgado were darkened by the shadows which crept out from the tired buildings.

The bank was closed—it looked like it was only open by appointment anyway—as was the general store. The saloons were booming.

Shelter swung down at the first he came to, noting with gratitude that there was a full water trough at the hitch rail. It had been a long dry day for the roan which had good breeding but obviously had gotten damn little exercise.

He loosened the cinches on the Texas-rigged saddle and let the roan drink. He dusted off his torn clothes and stepped up onto the swaying plankwalk before the saloon.

He waited until two men in work clothes came to the door and then he went in, keeping behind them. This was no time to start taking chances.

Inside Shelter was overwhelmed by a wall of noise. Glasses clinking, a piano, long out of tune banging away, raised voices, curses, poker chips falling. The atmosphere was blue smoky clouds. The sawdust underfoot was ancient, rancid with tobacco juice and vomit, beer and blood.

Maybe, he thought, those damned people in the citadel had something.

Two men dressed like cowhands argued at the long puncheon bar. Drunker than skunks, loud as a wounded bear, they continued their pointless argument as Shell walked slowly across the room, his eyes darting everywhere, searching the shadows, the smoke for one face. He could change his name but he couldn't change his face.

Morgan had Dabb's face engraved in his memory. He had had seven long prison years to relive that brutal ambush, to make a careful list of each man, writing down what he knew about them—where they had come from, what sort of work they preferred, every mole and scar he could recall.

He saw nothing at first look so he sauntered to the end

of the bar, out of the ring of light cast by the overhead lantern, and ordered a beer from the red nosed, big chested bartender.

"Have a tough crossing?" the bartender asked, looking Shell up and down. He needed a shave, wore torn jeans and shirt, still had the bandage on his arm.

"Might say that. Chiricahua."

"Bastards," the bartender muttered with no particular malice.

He was back in minutes with a frothing beer, yelling over his shoulder for the two drunken cowhands to shut up a minute. Shell slid a silver dollar over and got his change.

Shelter caught bartender's hand before he could turn away. "You know a man called Charles Dantworth?"

"Uh . . . not around here," he answered, but his eyes flashed a different message. He knew Dantworth. And he wasn't talking. The bartender shook away from Morgan and walked to the far end of the counter where the cowboys were calling loudly for liquor.

Shell sipped at the cool beer letting it trickle down his throat, parched and dusty from the long ride in. All right Dantworth or Dabb was around, or known here at the least.

Asking after the man was one sure way to get into trouble.

It was also the only way Morgan had of finding him And he meant to do that. Find this killer and have done with him.

"Hear you asking for somebody?"

The voice was at Morgan's shoulder and he turned to find a whiskered, hunched man beside him. His eyes glittered from a crinkled, walnut-colored face. He looked to

90

be a hundred and seven at the least.

"I was looking for a man."

"Dantworth?" the old man asked, bending forward, cupping a hand to his mouth.

"You got good ears."

"Make my living with them," he chuckled. "What's it worth to you?"

"It's worth a lot," Shell said, "but all I've got is the change from a lone silver dollar I've been carrying so long it was worn paper thin." Shell nudged the change on the bar. The old timer eyed it hungrily.

"That's it?"

"If I had more, I'd pay more."

"Ninety-five cents."

"Nineteen beers."

"Yeah," he said after counting on his fingers. "Now if you think of it, that's a hell of a lot for a little jawing, ain't it?"

"It beats getting nothing," Shell said. He stretched out a hand for his change and the old-timer stopped him.

"Wait. I reckon I know where he is. Come on, I'll even buy you another one," he said grinning toothlessly. "Harry—two more beers."

"You got ten cents?" the bartender asked suspiciously.

"I got it, damn you, I got it."

Shell grinned. The old man shoved over a dime, handed Shell a fresh beer and shot the bartender a withering glance. Harry the bartender just shrugged, dropping the change into his apron pocket.

"Over here, stranger," the old man said, and Morgan followed him to an empty table about the size of a flapjack, and they settled down into the creaky wooden chairs with the rattle and roar of loud conversation around them.

The old man took his time, first drinking half of the beer with unconcealed delight, licking the foam from his lips.

"It's Dantworth you want. Friend of yours?" he asked, leaning across the table.

"Acquaintance."

The old man laughed. "I knew it! You're after him, blast me. I can read your face, stranger."

"I was asked to look him up," Shell said evasively.

"Was you? I'll bet," the old timer said. Shell was wondering when if ever the man was going to get to the point. He took another healthy drink and then folded his arms on the table, looking at Morgan. "It's no secret, mister. Dantworth just don't like people asking after him. I know that because I seen a man get rousted out of town for asking the same question you're asking. Turned out he was a salesman who had a delivery for Dantworth, nothing more. Mister Dantworth, now, he's pretty nervous."

"Is he?"

"You don't know nothin' about that, I don't suppose?"

"Some folks are just naturally edgy," Shell replied.

"Yes," the old timer said drawling, "and some got reasons for being nervous."

"Could be."

"But you'll be wanting what you paid for." His voice dropped conspiratorially. "Dantworth's got a ranch outside of town. Ten miles south along the Rio Puerco. Got himself an army of men out there, supposed to be cowhands, but they ain't. Oh, Dantworth's got cattle enough, but most of them men he's got riding for him have never seen a cow off a platter. They got that look, friend.''

"What look?''

"What look? Why the look of a fighting man, same look as you got yourself. Only these boys they got them dead eyes—killers' eyes. Why they're nothin' but a private army. What he does with that army I couldn't say, but I'll tell you this, anyone that goes hunting Mister Dantworth and it ain't a friendly look-him-up . . . that fellow's got trouble, mister. You take my warning, 'cause it's God's truth. The man is mean and he's ready.''

Shell walked out of the saloon into the noisy, hazy night-darkened street. The roan looked up at him expectantly and Shelter crossed to where his horse was tied, stroking its neck thoughtfully.

There wasn't much more to be done that night. Shelter was broke and hungry, the horse hungry and weary. He slipped the reins from the hitchrail and started walking the street past the handful of cowboys—Dabb's men?—who were riding from one saloon to the next, sitting their saddles precariously.

He found the stable at the first cross street and walked the horse to it. Inside a withered, bald man of middle years sat thumbing through a dog-eared, torn copy of *Police Gazette*.

"Evening,'' Shell said.

"Put the pony up?'' the stableman asked without rising from the nail keg he was resting on.

"Maybe.'' Shell tilted back his hat. "If I can work it off.''

"Broke are you?''

"That's the word for it.''

"Well,'' he said, scratching his chin, "the boss don't

93

like it much, but if you feel like forking some hay dow
for me, shovelin' out a couple of stalls, I'll keep you bot
for the night.''

"I appreciate it.''

"It's nothin'. I been down on my own luck more'
once.''

Shelter got to it, forking down hay from the loft as th
stableman leafed lazily through his magazine. "Hov
about steady work?'' Shell called down.

"Here? Boss can't afford but one man and I got th
job, partner.''

"Not here, but I need something. Come morning th
horse will be fat but I'll be hungry enough to eat him.'

"What do you do?''

"Whatever there is to be done. Mostly cowhand.''

"Only ranch around is Double D.''

Double D. For Dantworth and Dabb? "Where's that?'

"Down the Rio Puerco, but I don't know if they'r
hirin'. Seems to me they got twice the men they'd nee
for what I've seen of the place. I haul hay out once in
while. Mister Dantworth ain't fixed too well for graze b
the time summer gets here.''

"But you think he might be hiring?''

"Mister, I don't think about Mister Dantworth at all i
I can help it. I don't care for him. Too highhanded to sui
me. But,'' he added, eyes narrowing, "from what I hea
you've got a better chance of hiring on out at Double D i
you can use that Colt you got strapped on.''

"That kind of outfit, is it?''

"It appears to be. But don't quote me. I don't knov
nothin', don't want to know.''

Shell lay awake in the loft long after the hostler ha
blown out his lantern and gone home. He leaned bac

against the straw bed he had fashioned for himself, hands behind his head, staring at the stars shining through the high window of the stable.

He knew where the man was.

Now just how in hell was he going to go about getting in there? What if he just rode out and asked to hire on? Would he be recognized? Dabb was the only one who could know who he was and likely the hiring was done by some middleman, the foreman. It would be an opportunity to look over the ranch, to locate Dabb, to plan an escape route.

It would also be an opportunity to get himself killed.

There was no point in thinking about it anymore on this night. Shell sighed, curled up on his straw bed and fell asleep, his stomach grumbling complaints, his dreams returning to a small, big-eyed girl in white robes.

With the dawn he was up, his eyes red, his blood trickling reluctantly through his veins. He climbed down the ladder to find the stableman in exactly the same position as the evening before, the same copy of the *Police Gazette* in his gnarled hands.

"Brought you some vittles from home. Figured you could use it," he said.

Morgan found a linen napkin sitting on the empty crate beside the hostler and with thanks, he opened it up to find two ham sandwiches. Thick slabs of well smoked ham between yeasty, fresh bread.

"There's coffee over there," the hostler said. He nodded toward the forge which apparently had been fired up on this warm morning just to keep the coffee pot hot. The hostler handed Shell a tin cup.

"Like I said," he told Shell, "I've been down on my luck a time or two."

"I'll pay you back for this," Morgan said around a mouthful of ham sandwich.

"Forget it." The stableman waved a hand. "Maybe sometime we'll meet again and I'll be the one without. For now, just eat up."

Shelter did, gratefully. When he was through the hostler asked, "Be moving on now, will you?"

"Unless you want me to work this off."

"No, forget it. Got plans, have you?"

"Yes," Shell said and his eyes went suddenly cold. The hostler recoiled involuntarily at the sharp-edged look which crept into those blue eyes. "I've got my plans. I appreciate the bed and the meal."

"Don't mention it."

The hostler retreated to his barrel and to his magazine, watching as the tall, blue-eyed man saddled his roan. Each move was purposeful, his jaw set, his eyes holding that hard gleam and the hostler knew that wherever this man was going there was someone who wouldn't be happy to see him arrive.

There was trouble in the wind. The stableman was only happy that it was blowing in another direction.

He stood, hands on hips, watching as the tall man in ragged clothes astride a high-stepping roan rode out into the sunrise-brightened streets of Delgado. Then with a sigh he turned back to his small, peaceful world.

Shell rode out of the west end of town, riding into the sagebrush country bordering the Rio Puerco. The morning was dry and warm, the river when he found it, only a sinuous silver band, three feet wide at most, running through the arid, sandy country flanking it.

In winter it might have been a fair sized river, but in the dead of summer it was only a withered lifeless ribbon of

96

water wandering aimlessly across the parched land.

Not the sort of river to support many cattle or much graze.

To the west, a series of low, broken hills, time-eroded and weathered, rocky and barren but for patches of nopal cactus formed a low bulwark against wandering cattle. Now Shelter was beginning to pass a few stray cows. They looked surprisingly sleek and fat. Grass, there was little, and what he saw was brown and chewed to the nub.

Cresting the low saddle he found the main ranch and it was an impressive sight. The Rio Puerco spread itself and watered perhaps a hundred acres of grass. It wasn't tall or flourishing at this time of year, still it was good graze for this part of the country.

Cottonwoods and oaks grew across the flat bottomland and a three-rail white fence enclosed a horse corral where dozens of blooded horses were held. They were the best money could buy, Kentucky blooded, the kind an outlaw favors. They'd run the hoofs off a mustang, and that was the whole idea.

Another quarter of a mile on was a low, spreading adobe house with a red tile roof, a long veranda and a neat if somewhat dry shrub garden before it.

Shell never reached the house.

Two men rode slowly toward him, each carrying a rifle across the saddlebows of his horse. They looked hard and prosperous. Both of them wore dark twill trousers, each had a new hat.

The man on the left was red-mustached, tall and scarred. He favored a pink and white striped shirt. The other one was sawed-off, dark, with a bulldog face and eyes of obsidian.

They halted and waited for Shell to draw even.

97

"Mornin', gents," Shell said, casually hooking a knee around his saddle horn. "I'm lookin' for work. This here's the only cattle outfit in the area they tell me, and so I wandered over. Where's the boss?"

"We ain't hirin'," the redhead said. His eyes swept over Shell inch by inch.

"Bascomb was looking for some people, Dewey," the squat, dark man said. Dewey was still eyeing Morgan.

"You don't look like no cowhand to me," he said to Shell.

Shelter grinned. "Maybe I look more like a banker?"

The short man looked at Shell's ragged clothes and laughed. "Shut up, Tabor," Red said.

"Ah, Christ, Dewey! He's just a man down on his luck, looking for a riding job. Send him over to Bascomb and let him decide it."

"Where the hell did you come from?" Dewey asked suspiciously. "Look, he don't even have a blanket roll."

"Well, I'll tell you," Shelter said, tilting his hat back. "I was with Señor Hernandez across the line in Nogales. We was driving north with a thousand head for the army at Fort Thomas, but the Chiricahua hit us. A dozen of us was killed, the cattle scattered all to hell. I took an arrow in the arm." He showed them the bandage. "Hernandez and those that was left pushed on. Them of us that was wounded was left behind. I holed up in Delgado for a while waiting for someone to pick me up, but no one came. Maybe they didn't get through. Anyway, here I am stranded, broke and hungry."

"Sounds right to me, Dewey," the short one, Tabor said.

"Anything sounds right to you."

"Hell, man's down on his luck. I know how it is, I

used to push cattle too, before . . ."

"Shut up." Dewey made up his mind. "You're in the wrong place. Go back up the creek until you come to a wagon road. Turn left and you'll come to a bunkhouse a mile on. Talk to a man called Bascomb."

"I appreciate it," Shelter said, touching his hat brim. Then he backed the roan and turned it up the creek, whistling as he rode. Dewey sat watching him.

"I don't like this one. Something about him—the eyes maybe."

"Christ, you're getting suspicious."

"That's what I'm paid for. One of these days that hombre the boss is looking for is going to show up."

"Yeah, but we can't turn away everyone that rides in."

"No. But this one . . . notice his horse didn't have a brand?"

"So, maybe they don't brand 'em down south of the border."

"And maybe this gent ain't never been to Nogales. Who the hell is Hernandez anyway? I never heard of no Mexican with a spread that big down there."

"That doesn't mean it ain't so."

"No, and it don't mean it is just cause he spins that yarn. I'm going to keep an eye on that man, Tabor. A real close eye, and when Mister Dantworth gets back, he'll decide."

"Liable to get your ownself in trouble, letting him stay on," Tabor said, starting to worry himself a little now. When Mister Dantworth got mad, he got real mad. Killing mad. Dewey looked at Tabor derisively.

"Changing your tune a little, aren't you? Don't worry, if I know Mister Dantworth, he'll give me a raise for keepin' this one around. If he's the one, Dantworth'll want him handy. No sense chasin' him down again just to kill him. No,'' Dewey turned his horse back toward the main house, ''if this is Shelter Morgan, we've got the bastard right where we want him.''

9.

Buck Bascomb was a man approaching fifty with wavy gray hair in profusion and a drooping gray mustache. His eyes were an alert green. His face was weather-tanned and lean. He listened patiently while Shelter repeated his fabricated story of the Mexican trail drive.

"It's a tough way to make a living," Bascomb commented when Shelter was through. "I've been stranded a time or two myself. Well, I guess they told you down below that I'm looking for some men. They're kind of hard to come by around here. We're isolated from the trails. Don't get too many cowhands wandering through—especially with the Apaches acting up. So, Mister . . . didn't catch the name."

"Charlie Hurt."

"Well, Charlie, I suppose we can take you on. I'll have to keep you around close for a few days. The boys are out on round-up in the Fortunas—that's them hills over there—so you'll be yard hand for a time. Looks like you could use some food and a set of clothes. Tall one, ain't ya? That a cow pony you got?''

"No, sir."

"Well, we'll mount you on something that knows cattle. By the way, don't call me sir. The boss, Mister Dantworth, he's 'sir'. Me, I'm Buck.''

He offered his hand and Shell took it, liking this cattleman with the weathered face and the alert eyes. Buck showed him the bunkhouse, empty now, and then took him into the adjoining kitchen where a wiry red-faced man named Teal was busy at the pots and pans.

"Fix this man some grub, Teal," Buck told him and the man nodded with the air of a martyr. "When you get done eating, Charlie, you come see me and I'll line you out."

"All right. Thanks, Buck."

The foreman grunted and went out, leaving Shell to stand in the kitchen while Teal cut a steak and fried it, throwing in potatoes and a few onions to keep the sirloin company.

Shelter ate at a small corner table, obviously Teal's private accommodations, thanked the cook and went out to find Buck Bascomb sitting on the front stoop of the bunkhouse, stitching a torn harness.

"Fill you up did he?" Buck asked. At Shell's nod, Bascomb said, "Well, Teal he's short on friendliness and maybe his cooking ain't the best, but you'll get it on time and you'll get plenty of it. Now then." He put the harness aside. "Let's you and me get a few things straight."

"All right," Shell agreed, folding his arms and leaning against the hitch rail.

102

"First off, I'm your boss. I don't take back talk."

"Wouldn't expect you to," Shell said easily and Buck loosened up a little.

"Some we've had do expect me to take it, Charlie." Buck went on. "Second, here's the way we operate. That down there," he nodded toward the big house, "is where the boss lives. No one goes down that way without the boss invites him. Understand?"

"There a reason for that, Buck?"

"Maybe a couple of reasons, but they don't concern you. I work for Double D, you work for me. You stay clear of the big house, Charlie."

"All right. If that's the way it is."

"That's the way it is. Come on now, I'll show you our working stock and you can pick one out. That roan is a beautiful animal, but if it ain't used to workin' cows it can get you killed. Next I'll dig up some clothes for you. You're kind of stretched out, but I think we can come close. Now and then a man takes off and don't come back. Maybe too much whisky in town then he feels like hitting the trail, maybe Apaches. Same as any ranch, though, we come up short now and again."

Shell managed to rummage through the pile of used clothes and come up with a maroon shirt and a pair of halfway decent jeans which dropped to his ankles. When he came out Buck nodded approval and said:

"Now you can start earning that chow and your bunk."

The woodpile was around back, ax stuck in the chopping block. "There's a stone over there to sharpen it if it needs it," Buck said with a nod. "Can you handle it with that arm?"

"It's mostly healed."

"All right. Do me up half a cord and stack it yonder." Buck nodded. "See you for supper."

Shelter yanked the ax free, tested the blade and found it wanting. He sharpened it to a fine edge and got to work, splitting the firewood. The sun rose higher and the sweat rained off of Morgan. He took off his shirt and placed it on the woodpile, pausing to stare down at the big house.

Was Dantworth there? he wondered. If not, where?

No matter, they would meet and soon. Shelter didn't like this set-up much, getting the man alone was going to be next to impossible.

He got to the wood. Holding the already sawn sections lengthwise on the chopping block, he split the logs into sections, his muscles working easily. Far from making his shoulder feel worse, it seemed to ease the soreness as his blood began to circulate, as the hot sun worked against his flesh.

He looked up, feeling eyes on him.

She was young, beautiful, Mexican. She wore a white blouse which slipped down off one shoulder, revealing the smooth coppery flesh. Her eyes were dark and laughing, her mouth a fluid, sensuous curve.

Her full breasts were high, her hips flaring and competent. She wore a dark skirt which the wind pressed against her thighs. She was simply standing in the shade of the big cottonwood tree, watching him.

"You bring me some wood too?" she asked finally, her accent velvety, caressing the English words.

"I don't know," Shell said, straightening to wipe his brow and grin at her. "Am I supposed to?"

"I think so." She smiled and it was a challenge and an invitation at once. She came nearer to Shell, hands clasped before her, her hips and shoulders swinging. "I think you should bring me some wood down to the big house.'' Her eyes were roving over him, taking in the hard, flat chest, the ropy muscles of Shell's shoulders.

"Uh uh," Shell said with a shake of his head. "I've been warned about that."

"About what, mister whats-is-it?"

"Charlie Hurt," Shell said, momentarily forgetting what his name was as he feasted his eyes on this lush and forward woman with the laughing eyes.

"Buck Bascomb don't tell you what to do, Mister Charlie Hurt. I say to bring the wood, you bring it."

"I'd have to check with Buck," Shell said. "This is my first day here. I'm not ready to lose this job just yet."

"Okay. You ask him. Tell him Carmalita wants wood brought to the kitchen at the big house. Okay?"

"Okay."

"Maybe later is better anyways. Maybe after supper, when it is dark, huh?" Her eyes gleamed meaningfully and Shell nodded slowly, still drinking in her beauty with his eyes. She seemed to enjoy it, seemed anxious to be appreciated. She was.

"I see you later then, Mister Charlie Hurt, okay?" she asked. She smiled deeply then, revealing even white teeth. Then she winked and slowly, deliberately turned away, her hips swaying compellingly as she walked back down the long slope toward the big house.

Later in the afternoon when Buck came to check on him, Shell gave the foreman Carmalita's message. Buck simply stared at Shell, slowly shaking his head.

"When the cat's away," Buck said sourly.

"What's up? This Carmalita married or something?"

"Something."

"She wanted it brought to the kitchen. I take it she's

105

the cook down there?''

"You take it wrong, Mister Hurt. What she is is poison. That's Carmalita Dantworth and she's the boss's wife.''

"His wife?'' Shell looked toward the house and then back to Buck. "What should I do, Buck?''

The foreman sighed. "If she asked for wood you'd better get it on down there, damnit. Wagon's around the back there.''

"She wanted it after supper, Buck.''

Buck looked at Shelter, his eyes growing cold. "You're playing with fire, boy.''

"I'm not playing with anything, Buck. I'm telling you what Carmalita asked for. I'm asking you what to do, that's all.''

"Yeah.'' Buck grumbled something else, spat and said, "Do like the lady asked, Charlie. Just do what she asked. But you watch yourself. You recall when I was telling you about some of the boys who worked here who just kind of wandered off and never came back?''

"Sure.''

Buck was still staring at the big house. Without looking at Shelter he said, "The word is that some of them didn't wander so damned far. Get me?'' He was still looking at the big house and Shell got him all right.

"I understand.''

"Stay clean if you want to stay healthy—a word to the wise, Charlie.'' Then grumbling still, Buck walked off. After a while Shell saw him ride out toward the Fortuna Mountains.

Morgan continued his work, his thoughts on Carmalita and the house below. Dangerous as hell it was. Carmalita was predatory and reckless. Yet Shelter needed to see the

106

house close up, to check the lay-out, to find out where Dantworth slept, where he worked, how many guns he had watching the place, to learn which windows were locked or barred, which doors might be left open. Now fate had tossed him the opportunity. He could do nothing about the few, exceedingly dangerous strings, which were attached.

A half dozen ranch hands showed up for supper which was eaten at a long plank table. One of these was the wrangler, a man named Harmon who was pleasant, blue-eyed and all of five feet tall.

Of the other four one was a man called Rufus Waite who had been tagged by a steer. The horn had torn open his thigh and killed the pony he was riding. Waite didn't look good, and there wasn't a doctor for two hundred miles. Before supper was over he fell off the long bench and two of the men carried him to his bunk where he would lie until he got well or died.

"Still going down there, are you?" Buck asked Shell later.

Buck and two other men were sitting on the porch in cane chairs, watching sunset spread a rosy glow across the broad land. "I suppose so," Shell replied. "The lady wants wood."

"I'm only glad it's you and not me," Harmon said with a grin. He was stoking up his pipe, his hat resting on his knee. "Though come to think of it, it just might be worth it."

Shelter had the wagon loaded already. He hitched the horses as darkness settled on the Double D. He would have to take the long way around. Although the main ranch house was less than a quarter of a mile from where he now stood, the road which wound along the creekbed was all of a mile, perhaps a little more.

It also meant that Shell would have to go past the sentries Dantworth had posted.

It couldn't be helped. He had to get down there, had to see what he was up against. He checked the loads in his Colt and holstered it. Beside him on the wagon bench was a pile of sacking and Shell slipped his rifle under it.

Then, as the first stars blinked on, as the mourning dove cooed from the cottonwood and the fire of sunset was washed out by purple night, Shell snapped the reins and walked the wood wagon forward, down the long creek trail, the men on the porch watching him with pity or curiosity or foreboding.

It was quiet along the creek. An owl dipped low over the meadow, chasing something Shell could not see. The creek was dark, silky, murmuring as Shell neared the front entrance to the main ranch, the wagon rumbling beneath him, his eyes searching the darkness, his mind flitting ahead to the dark-eyed, hungry, seductive Carmalita Dantworth.

It could easily be a set-up, Shell knew. It didn't have to be a deliberate plot to kill him, the thing could be done as easily by accident. Carmalita was a smoldering, sensuous woman, obviously unable to restrain her passions. Once Shelter was seen going near the house, wood wagon or not, someone would be around to keep an eye on him and report to Dantworth.

Or maybe not. Maybe they didn't report. Maybe they simply put the muzzle of a .44 to your head and squeezed the trigger.

"Halt! Who the hell are you and what are you doing?"

Shelter held up as the rider came out of the darkness, scattergun in his hands. He wore a dark slicker to merge with the night and rode a dark horse. He struck a match and leaned low out of the saddle to hold it under Shelter's chin.

Shell felt his muscles tense, his hand going slowly, automatically toward his holstered Colt.

"I don't know you."

"I just hired on today."

"Yeah?" he said suspiciously, allowing the match to extinguish itself. "I never heard of no hire-ons today."

"Ask Dewey or Tabor. They talked to me earlier. They're the ones who sent me up to Bascomb."

"Yeah?" the voice was still suspicious. The hammers of that double-ten the sentry was carrying were both drawn back. His eyes flickered to the wagon. "What's that you got there, firewood?"

"That's right. I'm supposed to take it to the kitchen—if you'd tell me where that is."

"I'll do better than that. I'll ride along with you."

"I appreciate it," Shell said innocently. He clicked the team into motion. "Boss back yet?" he asked casually.

"No he ain't. Say, didn't they tell you how things are around here?"

"What do you mean?" They were nearing the house now and Shelter could see upstairs windows lighted, see a guard walking a slow patrol around the house.

"What do I mean?" the guard laughed harshly. "It's this way, pal. This outfit down here is a different operation. You work for Bascomb, you stay away from the ranch. You punch cows and mind your own business."

"They told me that," Shell said. They were moving along a road toward the rear of the house. Overhead old sycamores stretched out black arms against the starlit sky.

"All right, then. You been told."

"It's just that I had the idea a man might make a little more money down here," Shell said with a wink.

"Did you now? You get all sorts of ideas, don't you?"

"I guess so. That's why I kind of wanted to talk to the boss as long as I was coming down here anyway."

"Well, he ain't here. Anyone hires on down below has to have references, pal. Understand me."

"No."

"If you don't you ain't cut out for this. Stick to punching cows, pal. It'll save you a lot of grief."

They were at the back door to the house now, the kitchen entrance Shell supposed. He was gauging the strength of the door, mentally measuring the height of the balcony which overhung it, guessing how well anchored into the adobe the bars over the upstairs windows were.

The door opened and she stood there outlined by the light within. Full, ripe, cordial.

"Come in, Mister Hurt. Come in and bring the firewood. Daltry," she said to the guard, "away, hombre. Why you think Carmalita needs a keeper?"

"That's exactly what I think," he muttered. Aloud he said, "I thought I'd help this man unload the wood, Miz Dantworth."

"No. Go on about whatever you do. He is a strong man, no? He can do what must be done himself."

10.

Still muttering, his face dark with resentment, Daltry turned his horse and slowly walked it back toward the front of the big house.

"Come in," Carmalita said, waving her hand, "come in Mister Hurt."

"Maybe it's be better if I got some wood first," Shell replied dryly. Lord, that was a woman. She had brushed her hair to a blue-black sheen. She wore a simple white dress which barely restrained the eager breasts, which did nothing to conceal the long line of her thighs, the swell of her hips.

Shell stacked an armload of wood, and went to the kitchen door, easing in sideways, eyeing the wide kitchen with the huge stone fireplace, the copper kettles, the door which opened onto a long lighted corridor beyond. Through that Shell could see a staircase leading to the upstairs rooms.

Shell put the wood down in the corner and turned. She was against him suddenly, drawing his hand to her hip, parting her lips as she kissed him, her breath coming quickly.

"Upstairs, Mister Hurt. Upstairs."

Shell gently unwound her. "Uh uh," he said, smiling.

"But why? I am a woman who knows much, who needs much, who can give much."

"You're also a woman who can get me killed, Carmalita."

Her hands rested on his thighs, and now they began to work slowly up and down, her thumbs touching his crotch as she smiled up at him with those glowing eyes.

"My husband is not at home."

"Where is he?"

"I don't know," she said with a hint of anger. "Business. Always he is away on business. I do not know where he goes and I do not care. I am glad when he goes."

Her hands had continued to creep up and now they cupped Shell, hefting him, measuring him. *"Ay, muy hombre,"* she whispered. "I am a woman who knows how to use it."

"I'll bet you are, but not here, not now."

"Why? Why not, Mister Hurt?"

Shell stepped around her and walked toward the door again. Before he reached it Daltry appeared, shotgun still in his hands, "That's why," Shell thought. He brushed by the cold appraising Daltry and went to the wagon, returning with the second armload.

Carmalita, bending to pick up a fallen stick of wood whispered, "I do not give up so easily, Mister Hurt."

112

Daltry was still watching. Shell made no response whatever. Two more trips and he was finished.

"You get yourself back up to the bunkhouse now, Hurt," Daltry ordered and Shelter touched his hat brim.

"I was meaning to. Good night, Mrs. Dantworth."

When he stepped into the wagon box and unwound the reins from the whipstock she was still watching, arms folded beneath her breasts, eyes gleaming with sensuality. Shell decided it would be a rough night.

After some tossing and turning he managed to get to sleep in the stale bunkhouse despite the heavy snoring and the taunting images of Carmalita, the tactile memory of her hands, her warm, pliant lips.

In the morning he rolled out when everyone else did to face the cool, gray pre-dawn world.

Finding Buck, Morgan asked: "Am I going to see some cows today, Buck?"

"No." His response was a growl.

"What the hell's the matter? I do something?"

"I don't know, Charlie, did you?" He handed Shell a folded piece of paper and turned, stalking away, his leather heels clicking across the bunkhouse floor.

Shell shrugged and opened the note.

Mister Bascomb,

Please send to me the Charlie Hurt this morning to help me in going to town with my packages and the driving.

                    S. Carmalita Dantworth

"Well, she said she didn't give up easily," Shell said to himself. Then, shaking his head he walked in to eat

113

breakfast, ignoring the amused, somewhat contemptuous—jealous?—glances of the others around the table.

He decided to walk the quarter of a mile down the hill to the big house, a decision that would have made a proper cowboy blanch. Those boys wouldn't walk across the street if their horse was handy.

Shell had other reasons than the exercise. He wanted to see if it could be done, if a man could slip up on the house unseen from this side. After all, if Dantworth expected trouble, and apparently he did, this side was the least likely.

Shelter started through the low oaks and paused, looking downslope toward the big adobe house. There was a draw to his right, and it seemed that if a man kept his head down he would have a chance of coming up behind the house unseen. There would be fifty yards of open ground left to traverse, but at night it could be done. Or so he hoped.

Shelter walked down the draw, the dawning sun warm and brilliant. He kicked out a skittering cottontail, pausing to watch it bound away and nearly stepped on an early-rising rattlesnake which continued on its way sketching a sinuous line across the little used path.

Emerging from the draw he walked directly to the house and knocked loudly on the kitchen door. There was no answer despite the fact that Shelter could hear pots being banged around, low, cheerful Spanish voices.

Good. That would give him a chance to see the front of the house a little more closely. He strolled along the shaded path and was challenged as he rounded the corner to the front of the house.

"Stop right there." It was Dewey, the red haired man Shell had run into the day before. "Where in hell did you

114

me from?''

"The bunkhouse.''

"How? I didn't see nobody.'' Dewey's eyes narrowed
spiciously.

"Hell, Dewey, I walked right down the hill. You
ould have seen me.''

"Maybe. What do you want anyway?''

Shell pulled the note from his pocket and handed it to
ewey who was wearing a duster despite the heat of the
orning. Dewey took the note with his left hand. His
ght was busy cradling that rifle he favored. He looked at
ell and shook his head.

"No dice, Hurt.''

"Why not?''

"Why the hell you think not? The boss don't want any
you cowboys prowling around down here. If Carmalita
ants to go to town she's got old Juan to drive her buggy.
e don't need you for nothing. Get.''

"All right.'' Shelter shrugged and started to turn away.
ne voice from the front door called out angrily.

"What you doing now, Dewey! What you think I am,
prisoner of this house, damn you! I am the señora. This
my rancho. This man, he works for me. Do your busi-
ss somewhere else, Dewey, I am angry at always hav-
g you stupid men doing what I don' like.''

"It's what the boss don't like, Carmalita,'' Dewey
id calmly.

"Well what I like counts. I am the señora. You are just
pistolero. No or si?''

"Whatever you say, Carmalita,'' Dewey said reluc-
ntly. He looked at Shell, dark eyes peering out from be-
ath bushy red eyebrows. "You watch your ass, Hurt,''
 said under his breath. "I'd keep my horse saddled was

115

I you.''

He handed the note back to Shell and spun away, con
tinuing his rounds. Carmalita, hands on hips, let loose
long, triumphant laugh.

"Come in, Charlie Hurt, come into *mi casa*."

Shelter walked that way. Carmalita stood at the head c
the tile steps, wearing a silk dressing gown, her dark hai
flowing across her shoulders, her black eyes glittering
Her hands were on her magnificent hips, her wrapper fe
slightly open at the neck as she welcomed Shell and h
saw that she had nothing on underneath. He could see th
beginning of the generous, healthy breasts beneath th
wrapper and he couldn't help staring.

Carmalita laughed. "I thought you did not like Carma
lita, Mister Hurt.''

"I like Carmalita all right. I just don't like gettin
shot," Shell told her, and she laughed again. She was
bold, bawdy, handsome woman who would live heartil
until she died and Shelter admired her. He was als
damned wary.

"Come in." She took his arm and nudged him with
breast, leading him through to the interior of the bi
house. The small foyer led to a high ceilinged front roon
which was done up with massive, black wood Spanis
furniture. A gun collection hung on the walls, everythin
from ancient wheel locks to Springfield breech loaders
from gold-chased H & H safari rifles to blunderbusses.

"Your husband likes guns," Shell commented casu
ally.

"Yes. Guns and money. Not much else does he like.'
Carmalita led him to the foot of the staircase which wa
balustraded with massive dark wood pillars. "I mus
dress. Come up and talk to me while I dress, Miste

116

Hurt..

"I think I'll stay downstairs," Shell said, and Carmalita laughed again. Her hand lingered on his shoulder for long moment and then slipped onto the bannister.

"All right. You have a drink, Juan will show you where."

Shelter turned to see the withered, sour-faced servant standing behind him where he would have heard all. A drink was the last thing Shelter wanted at this time of the morning, but it would give him a chance to poke around.

Shell watched Carmalita move slowly up the staircase, her hips straining at the silky blue fabric of the wrapper she wore. She was all woman, this one, always aware of the impression she made on men, of the power she wielded with that body.

"Come on, Juan. Show me where the liquor is."

Juan made no reply. He turned and shuffled toward another room, Shelter striding behind him, looking at the heavy furniture, the expensive rugs, the lavish panelling.

Dabb had done all right for himself. He had invested his share of the blood money in a fine house, a nice ranch, a beautiful wife. Shell wondered if it ever bothered him, if Dabb ever woke up in a cold sweat in the middle of the night, seeing hands reach out for him from out of the snow, seeing the blood, the frozen bodies, the hollow-eyed, hungry ones.

He doubted it. Dabb's kind seldom did. They had somehow gotten the idea that they were the center of the universe, that the thousands of years of civilization, the lives of millions of people, the work many hands had done had all been for their benefit, that they were the final aim of time and the finest triumph of civilization.

Shell entered the study behind Juan. Books lined the

117

walls, a liquor sideboard nestled among them. Shelter had the idea the liquor was used a hell of a lot more than the books, all of which had leather bindings and gold leaf embellishments.

Juan nodded toward the liquor and then turned away, shuffling out again, his thoughts unreadable. Shelter walked to the liquor cabinet, glanced around to assure himself that Juan was out of the room, and then turned, going to the massive desk which sat near the high, red-draped window.

The drawers were all locked and Shell decided not to jimmy them. There was a pile of papers on Dantworth's desk however, and Morgan shuffled through them, his eyes flickering frequently to the open doorway.

Dantworth had strange interests for a cattleman. There was not a word to be seen about graze or the new breeds, about horses, animal diseases. The papers were newspaper clippings and articles from financial magazines. Railroad bulletins.

Shell glanced at them all. There was an announcement concerning the new bank in Socorro, the word 'Socorro' now circled in black ink. A bulletin from the Southern Pacific advertised for agents to operate whistle stop facilities along a new line to be built from Fort Bowie to Tubac in southern Arizona. The Four Strike Mine in the Dragoon Mountains was advertising for laborers and announcing to its stockholders that Four Strike expected to pay an extraordinary dividend on its million-dollar profit for the preceding year.

Yes, Mister Dantworth had extraordinary interests.

At the bottom of the stack Shell found a very recognizable sketch of James R. Dewey, alias Red Chambers, alias Alabama Red, wanted for robbery and murder.

118

Dewey's 'references', no doubt.

"Have you found something interesting?" the mocking, familiar voice asked from the doorway.

Shell let the stack of papers fall back onto the desk. "No. Just nosy, I guess, Carmalita."

"So was I once, but it is not too healthy to be so interested in my husband's business affairs."

"No. I guess not."

"You are ready now?" she asked. And Shell walked to her, noticing with approval the long buckskin skirt, the filmy white blouse, the scent of her which reminded him of mountain lilac.

"I'm ready," he said, meaning it.

The carriage was ready and waiting before the house, Juan dispassionately holding the reins as Shell helped Carmalita Dantworth up onto the seat then stepped up himself.

Across the yard Shell could see Dewey standing, scowling, that rifle in his hands. He ignored the gunman, took the ribbons from Juan and snapped the reins, moving the black Tennessee walker out at a brisk pace while Carmalita, leaning back against the seat laughed and threw out a joyous arm.

"Freedom," she cried. "Anytime I leave this place it is like the world is born again."

"Why'd you marry him?" Shell asked. The horse had settled into an even ground-devouring pace. The country flitted past, dry, sun-yellowed, wild.

"Do you know what poverty is?" Carmalita asked. She shrugged. "I have seven brothers and sisters and no father. This man came and would have me. I married him."

"Like that."

"Like that. Take that road over this hill. It is much shorter."

Shell doubted it, but he turned the horse up the narrow trail which ran up along the side of a grassless knoll.

Reaching the crest, Carmalita put a hand on his wrist. "Wait here for a minute, Mister Hurt."

Shell reined up and Carmalita swivelled in the seat, squinting down the backtrail for long minutes. "No one is following," she said eventually.

"You're very careful."

"I have learned this," Carmalita said with a touch of uncharacteristic bitterness creeping into her words. "Drive on, Mister Hurt. I think maybe we are too early for all the shops to be opened. I think we should wait for a little while."

Shell said nothing. He followed Carmalita's instructions, driving over the knoll and up a shadowed canyon where rife cottonwood draped shadows across the narrow road. A pleasant little creek burbled down through the rocks beside the road. At the head of the canyon the creek temporarily widened.

"Here, stop please," Carmalita said.

Shell nodded, looking around. The canyon walls rose high on three sides. The cottonwoods and willows were thick. The creek ponded here before tumbling on down the rocky canyon to rejoin the Rio Puerco somewhere out on the desert.

"A beautiful spot, is it not?" Carmalita asked. Her eyes were strangely soft. Her lower lip drooped heavily, beneath the fragrance of her lilac powder Shell could scent a richer, sexual perfume.

"I must take my bath here," Carmalita said, casually unbuttoning her blouse. She performed the ritual slowly,

120

her fingers caressing each button as the full brown breasts were gradually exposed, as Shell's pulse began to rise. "Maybe you want to turn your back," she said playfully. "Maybe you want to sit over there in the shade so that you don't see Carmalita."

"Maybe I don't," Shell said.

Carmalita laughed. She laughed and shrugged out of her blouse. She had worn nothing underneath. Her firm, ripe breasts bobbed free, taut dark nipples jutting proudly toward Shell.

"Is naughty?" she asked, cupping her breasts, holding them up for Shell's admiration.

"Very."

"I think so too," she said. Already her fingers were working on the buttons of her skirt and now it too fell away and Shell's eyes caressed the dark beauty of her thighs, the honey-colored buttocks, the dark flourishing down between her legs.

"Come," she said. Her finger crooked. "Come see what is naughty."

Shell looped the reins around the whipstock and slipped to the ground. Carmalita was in his arms suddenly. Sun-warmed, ripe, eager. She guided his lips to her breasts, sighed as his tongue traced patterns around her nipple, let her hands drop urgently to his belt.

She worked hastily, finally getting the buckle undone, slipping his trousers down as her hands found Shell, encircled him, as her breath caught and she lifted herself onto tiptoes, rubbing against him, trying to fit him to her.

"Just a minute," Shell said with a laugh. He rapidly removed his shirt and boots and kicked off his trousers.

Turning he saw that Carmalita had gone into the stream. She was leaning against a tilted, water-polished rock and the silver water ran in an undulating film across her body as she sat, arms stretched out, watching Shell who dipped a toe into the creek and then entered the crystal water to lie beside her.

Her arms enveloped him and her legs spread eagerly as Shelter rolled to her, feeling the clasp of arms and thighs. He slid easily into her and he felt her shudder with delight, heard her murmuring encouraging words in English, in Spanish, in a language which had no meaning outside of the world of lovemaking.

Carmalita was passionate and strong, her sturdy, accomplished hips rising and falling eagerly, her pelvis nudging his as she teased her body to fulfillment. Her strong, sleekly muscular thighs wrapped around Shell's waist and she continued to murmur, to bite at his shoulders, to claw at his back as the cool water rushed over them frothing and seething as Caramlita seethed, as she rushed over Shell, devouring him until her throat emitted a clear, birdlike cry and she fell back, petting him, kissing his muscular chest, her body quivering with residual tremors.

Shell stroked her damp dark hair and relaxed in her arms. After a time he asked, "Carmalita, can I ask you something."

"Yes?"

"It's about your husband."

"You are worried?"

"It's not that. I'd like to know something about his business."

"You did not find out all from the papers on his desk?"

"I'd like to know more."

She was silent for a moment, her fingers still running

up and down Morgan's spine. "No," she said eventually. "I will tell you nothing."

"Why? I got the idea you didn't love him much."

"I hate him. He is a pig."

"Then?"

"He is a pig, but he is the man who supports me. Who gives me money to send to my family in Mexico. It is through him I live."

"Not much of a life, is it?" he asked. He lifted his head and looked into those dark, thoughtful eyes. She shook her head slightly.

"It is a good life. Before it was very bad. What you think, Mister Hurt, whatever your name, that because you have laid me down and give me pleasure that I am in your power? Carmalita makes love for the joy of it, and she gives pleasure. She is not a slave to no man."

"That's not the way I was thinking."

"No? You won't ask about Mister Dantworth.

"No."

"But you will make love again?" she asked. Shelter nodded and she laughed out loud, pulling his mouth to hers, her body again beginning that slow pulsing as the stream flowed away and the sun floated high in a clear white sky.

11.

Delgado slept in the morning sunlight, looking dry, dead and dusty. There were several horses in front of the saloons, but little traffic on the street. Shelter saw a kid with a fishing pole over his shoulder, a sleepy yellow dog in the center of the street, a storekeeper sweeping the plankwalk before his shop, two ladies walking arm in arm toward the bank. That was it. The sum total of the activity in Delgado on this weekday morning.

"Over there," Carmalita directed. "That is the mercantile store. I have to shop there."

Shelter nodded. He had the idea that most of the shopping would be for necessities to send to her family below the border. She looked just fine. She had pinned her dark hair up and the hot wind had dried it quickly.

She smiled up at him as he helped her from the buggy. "I will be a long time, Mister Hurt. Why don't you have a beer in the saloon.''

Shell wasn't much of a beer drinker, but the day was hot and there wasn't much else to do in Delgado. He took the silver dollar Carmalita fished out of her purse, figuring it for an advance on his pay.

With a soft smile she was gone, greeting the store keeper cheerfully. Shelter left the buggy hitched there and crossed the street to the Golden Eagle, the town's busiest saloon.

It was too early for even the hardcase regulars, and Shell had the place practically to himself. He took the beer to a corner table where he could see out onto the street and watch for Carmalita, although she wasn't the shy type to stand out there in the street waiting for her driver. She'd bust on into the saloon, ignoring the ''Ladies not Served'' signs.

Shell placed his hat on the table and leaned back, feeling relaxed and easy. The beer was cool, the interior of the saloon dark and quiet. The heat of the day hadn't managed to reach the inside of the buildings yet. Two old timers played poker for matches across the way. A teamster was swapping tales with the bartender as he cleaned up behind the counter.

It couldn't last long, this feeling of contentment. Shell gazed out the window, at the distant mountains, the broad desert, knowing that soon Charles Dantworth would be riding back from one of his ''business trips'', that soon the guns would blaze and men die.

For now, however, he stretched out his legs and crossed them at the ankles, sipping the beer as the morning lagged.

He watched the street, seeing a freight wagon roll in, two cowboys standing on the corner betting on a dog fight. A man with silver hair who wore a bright red cravat with a brown suit strolled past and Shelter followed him with his eyes for a way.

There was something about that one . . . he sat upright suddenly, pushing his beer mug away.

Brother Thomas!

The storekeeper from the citadel was in town, walking casually down the boardwalk. That freight wagon must have been driven by him.

It had taken Shelter a time to recognize him. In a brown town suit he looked like another fairly prosperous merchant. Shell craned his neck, trying to follow Thomas, but he was out of his line of vision.

He shrugged and settled back in his chair. Should he say hello to him, ask about Freida? What point was there in it?

Funny about that suit. Shelter supposed it would raise too much curiosity if Brother Thomas came into town wearing white robes. He finished his beer and stood. Why not say hello; Shell was doing nothing else worth doing.

He pushed on through the saloon door and went out into the street. The day was so hot it was difficult to breathe. The sun was penetrating, harsh. The dogs had stopped their fighting and now lay in uneasy peace ten yards from each other, panting in the shade.

Shelter walked toward the mercantile, figuring that Thomas had to have gone there, but there was no man in the store. Only two older women and Carmalita who waved and displayed ten fingers.

Ten minutes before she was ready. That would be the minimum.

Shelter turned and walked out through the green door,

squinting into the harsh sunlight. He glanced toward the stable, wondering if he ought to saunter over there and again thank the hostler for the bed and the meal.

He saw him again.

Brother Thomas, or someone awfully like him, wearing a brown suit and brown hat, striding down the alley between the stable and the hardware store.

Shelter walked that way, curiosity building. He crossed the street and craned his head around the corner of the hardware store. Nothing. Thomas had gone on.

"Where in hell does a monk go on his day off?" Shell grumbled.

He didn't like this suddenly. He knew that Brother Thomas came into town occasionally, knew that he must wear something other than his robes. But what in hell was he up to, sneaking down alleys?

"Probably nothing, Morgan," he told himself. "Maybe he buys a bottle of whisky and drinks it down." The problem was Shelter had lived too long in a world where people had devious motives. He had not learned to be particularly trusting.

He moved into the alley, his hand now resting on the butt of his Colt.

He could hear voices now from the far end of the alley. He could see nothing. Beyond the walls of the buildings the empty desert spread toward the Fortunas, lost in a heat haze.

What in hell was going on here?

He eased toward the end of the alley, pausing just around the last corner. From there he could hear the soft voices. Thomas and another voice somehow familiar which Shell couldn't put a face to.

"All right then, it will be ready."

"Right after sundown."

"That's what I said, isn't it?"

"Mister Dantworth will want it all to be right."

"I told you it would be, didn't I?" This was Brother Thomas, irritable and tense.

Shell had finally placed the other voice. It belonged to Dewey, the gunhand from the Double D. Just what in hell were the two men talking about?

"What else," Shell said under his breath. A horde of gold money. What else would be of interest to Charles Dantworth? Brother Thomas had sold out. Beneath his monkish robes had beat a little avaricious heart, one which couldn't bear seeing that gold coin buried with the "saints". The others had been locked away in that citadel for years, praying and fasting. Brother Thomas had been coming out into this pagan world, maybe developing a taste for whisky and women. Maybe he had started gambling and losing—who knew? But he was about to play Judas, except there was a hell of a lot more than thirty silver pieces at stake.

Shelter turned and started back up the alley, his mind racing ahead of him. It was a moment before he was aware of the two men blocking his path.

He recognized neither of them, but he recognized their cut immediately. Both were tall, both unshaven. Both had rifles in their hands. Their eyes were on Shelter. Hard cold eyes, dead eyes, killing eyes.

Shell flung himself to one side, and as he did so the rifles spewed flame. Bullets tore into the clapboard behind his head, tearing out huge chunks of wood.

Shell's Colt was already to hand. He fired as he fell, and landing, he rolled prone and touched off again. The first man was tagged hard. The .44 nearly blew his head off and he flew backward, arms outflung, his rifle dropping uselessly to the ground.

The other badman took off at a run and Shelter winged a shot at him. He crumpled and went down, clasping his leg. He got up again, abandoning his rifle, and limped around the corner onto the main street. Shelter pursued.

Before he reached the head of the alley the other man had stepped into it, casting a long, blocky shadow.

"Hold it right there," he said softly, and Shelter, seeing the ten-gauge in his fists, the star hanging from his worn leather vest, did just that.

Shell slowly raised his hands, dropping the Colt on the sheriff's order. Behind the big man now was a milling crowd. They peered around the sheriff, looking at the man with the shattered skull who lay dead in the alley, already drawing buzzing blue flies.

"We've got some talking to do," the sheriff said. He gestured with his shotgun and Shell started forward. "Get the hell back!" the lawman shouted at the crowd and they dispersed rapidly.

Shell walked down the main street, followed by the sheriff. People stopped what they were doing and watched from the plankwalks.

"Here," the sheriff said, and Shell turned into a falsefronted, off-green building which had bars on the windows. The inside of the building was hot and sour. Someone in back was snoring loudly. "Keep on walking," the sheriff said.

"I thought we were going to talk about this."

"We will, later." There was no smile on the lawman's broad, ox-like face.

Shell shrugged and walked toward the back of the building, seeing the twin cells with iron bars. A drunk was sleeping half on, half off a wall-hung cot.

Morgan was shown his own accommodations.

The cell was small, windowless, tightly barred. "I get damned tired of you cowboys coming into town and shooting each other to dog meat," the sheriff said.

His name was Ruben Proxmeyer and he was something of a rarity—a twenty-year law man. In a time and place where lawmen were gunned down from ambush, lynched by their own constituency and challenged each and every night at saloon closing time, the rate of attrition was extremely high in Proxmeyer's business.

He had hung on this long by being careful and by letting everyone know that he meant business. This attitude had led to the development of a perpetual scowl, a bad case of ulcers and grudging respect from all quarters of society.

"They came after me, Sheriff," Morgan said as Proxmeyer turned the iron key in the cell door and returned the key to his pocket.

"Self-defense?"

"That's right."

"Yeah. There must have been one killing around here in the last five years that wasn't self-defense, but I can't recollect it."

"Take a look. They shot up the walls of the hardware store pretty good trying to get me."

"That doesn't mean they shot first," Proxmeyer snapped.

"There was two of them. Think I challenged two men?"

Proxmeyer looked his prisoner up and down. "I wouldn't doubt it a bit."

"What happens next?" Shelter asked.

130

"Next?" Proxmeyer scratched his jaw. "I suppose they might have a trial of some sort. Then you learn to do some neck dancing."

"It was self-defense!"

"Like I said, it always is. They always hang anyway. Folks around here kind of like a nice hanging to sort of liven things up."

With that Proxmeyer was gone and Shell sagged onto the cot. The drunk continued his fluttering snores.

Shell circled the cell with his eyes, seeing no weak spots. Casually, glancing toward Proxmeyer's office door, he went to the bars and tested them with his hands, straining with shoulders and legs. Nothing moved but Shell's popping ligaments and muscles.

He was stuck. And meanwhile Dantworth was planning a raid on the citadel. Morgan was sure that that was what Brother Thomas and Dewey had been talking about.

And why not? What other job offered so much hard cash for so little risk? The people out there weren't going to fight back. Even if they had the will to, they had no weapons. It was going to be like taking candy from babies.

Shelter had a sudden, heart stopping thought. Why would Dantworth leave any of them alive? No one even knew those people existed. No one would miss them, and there would be no witnesses, no one to complain that they had been robbed. Only a cavern full of bones. The perfect job.

"I've got to get out of here!" Shell slammed the heel of his hand against the bars. The drunk's snoring faltered and sputtered. "Sheriff! I've got to talk to you!"

And tell him what? That out on the desert a hundred men and women were living in the heart of a hollowed-out mesa, and that the biggest local rancher, who was actually an outlaw, was going to ride out there and kill them all for a cache of gold a mysterious benefactor had given them. Shell wouldn't believe it himself except he *knew*. He knew the people involved, knew what and who Charles Dantworth was.

"Sheriff!"

There was no answer at all. Shelter paced the floor of his cell like a caged animal. Damnit, a hundred people were going to die if he didn't get out of here! A hundred gentle, harmless people who were targeted only because they had some rare metal in their possession, a cache of yellow gold which they didn't give a damn about.

"Sheriff!"

Again there was no answer and Shelter could only walk to his cot and sag onto it, staring at the floor. Wouldn't this give Dabb a belly laugh? Morgan held in jail and hung because he had fought off two hired killers?

The law would do his work and Dabb would come off clean again. Free to continue doing what he had been—hiding behind his pose as a respectable cattleman while his army of gunhands roved the southwest, killing and robbing.

What was it about gold? Shell had wondered at it time and again. With a single exception each of those men who had ambushed them in that Georgia woods all those years ago had continued their life of crime. They had never been satisfied, never seen enough gold or blood. It seemed to become an obsession, a quite deadly obsession.

Shelter came to his feet, hearing conversation in the sheriff's office. He smiled, recognizing the voice which became clearer as Sheriff Proxmeyer led the way to the

132

holding cell.

"Is a terrible thing," Carmalita said loudly. "These hombres come out to wave guns in our faces and Mister Hurt is fighting them while Carmalita runs away to make her escape!"

"Yes, Mrs. Dantworth," Sheriff Proxmeyer said wearily.

"And you put Mister Hurt in the jail! It is a crime. He was a-heroic!"

"Yes, Mrs. Dantworth," the sheriff said. "Tell me again what happened."

"I tol' you! These mans come for us and I think they will do something terrible and they start a-shooting at Mister Hurt and he fires back bravely. I ran because I was very scared and when I come back I find that you have taked Mister Hurt away to lock him up."

They had halted before the cell door, Carmalita sparing a surreptitious wink for Shell.

"Thing is, Mrs. Dantworth, that dead man—well, someone identified him as one of your husband's cowboys."

"Is impossible! I never see him before. If he was my husband's man he was a crazy one who comes after me while my husband is away." Carmalita's voice was excited, but her eyes were calm and mocking. "I want you to let this man out. *He* works for my husband and has saved my life."

Proxmeyer looked like he believed this. As much as he believed the man in the moon. Nevertheless he had a witness, and a prominent witness. He fished the key from his pocket and unlocked the cell door, swinging it wide to let Shell out.

"Come, Mister Hurt," Carmalita said, hooking her

arm around his, "we must get back to the ranch. I must lie down and rest after this."

"In a minute, Mrs. Dantworth," Shell replied, checking out the Colt which Proxmeyer returned to him before holstering it. "I want to talk to the sheriff."

"We've got nothing to talk about." Proxmeyer settled heavily into his chair.

"It's not about this shooting, sheriff. I stumbled onto something and it could involve the lives of a lot of people."

"Oh?" Proxmeyer managed to stave off a yawn.

"Yes. I want you to listen to me, and listen closely." With that Shelter plunged into the story of the citadel, the buried gold, the meeting between Brother Thomas and Dewey. The sheriff listened, his expression ranging from disinterest to bald skepticism.

"You expect me to believe that?" Proxmeyer asked when Shelter was finished. "I never heard such a far-fetched bucket of hogwash in my life."

"It's true. Every word of it," Shell said hotly.

"Is it?" Proxmeyer grunted. "All those folks living out there in the mesa, are they? And no one knew anything about it until you stumbled onto it. And Mister Dantworth is really a hold-up artist. And you want me to ride out there into Chiricahua country to stop this. Mister, you don't deserve to hang—you need to be locked up in an asylum. Look, partner, even if I did believe you, and I don't, not in the slightest, I can't to wandering out there. It's out of my jurisdiction. I'm going to do you a favor and let you walk out that door, crazy as you are. Now do me one, and get!"

"That's your final word?"

Proxmeyer rose to his feet angrily. "Damnit, Hurt,

you're getting to me now. I asked you to get. You don't and I'll drum up some charge to throw you back in that cell. Understand me?''

"I do." Shell stood across the desk from Proxmeyer, his jaw muscles twitching. Damn the man! Couldn't he even spend half a day to find out if there was any truth in what Morgan was saying.

"Please," Carmalita touched Shell's arm. "Let us go, Mister Hurt. Maybe you bang your head back in the alley, huh?"

She tugged at him, drawing him toward the door. Shell planted his feet and halted. There was one more question he wanted to ask.

"Sheriff, have you ever heard of a man called Cassius Dormer?"

The sheriff actually blanched. His expression faded to blank puzzlement.

"Cassius Dormer? Hell yes, I've heard of Cassius Dormer? The question is where in hell did you hear about that? Just what kind of snake pit have you gotten yourself tangled up in, Mister Hurt?"

The sheriff took a long time composing himself. He fished in his desk drawer for a half cigar which he lit slowly, ceremonially. Carmalita's hands had fallen away and there was no sound but the steady fluttering snore of the drunk in the cell.

Shelter leaned against the wall, waiting patiently. The name had triggered something unexpected in the sheriff, a thoughtful, reflective mood and Shell settled in to hear just what the sheriff did know about Cassius Dormer, the Benefactor, the source of the citadel's wealth, the key to all of this fantastic mystery.

12.

"Let me get this straight," Sheriff Proxmeyer said, jabbing at Shelter with his stubby cigar, "are you saying that Mrs. Dantworth's husband was tied up in that Cassius Dormer business?"

"No. In fact I don't think he was," Shell answered. "But Cassius Dormer is involved in this somehow."

"I don't see how," Proxmeyer said, leaning back in his chair. "The man's been dead for ten years."

"Who is this man?" Carmalita asked. She looked from Shell to Proxmeyer, waiting for an answer. It was the sheriff who had to explain it to both of them.

"Shortly before the war a man named Cassius Dormer visited Arizona on a combination business and hunting trip. Now if you don't know his background, I'll tell you this. The Dormer family was aristocratic Baltimore at its best. The old man—Cassius Dormer's father, that is—is ied into railroads, coal and steel. Big money, if you know what I mean. The kind men like us can't even imagine.

"Dormer was supposedly on a hunting trip, but word was around that he was scouting a rail line through to the west coast, which is probably accurate although the line was never built because of the cost and the Union Pacific competition.

"Anyway, to cut a few corners, one night a dozen or so men broke into the Dormer camp outside of Tucson and after one hell of a gunfight they made off again with Cassius Dormer."

"They snatched him."

"That's right. His father was notified immediately and a reward of ten thousand dollars was posted—that's how I came to know about this. Ten thousand dollars, by God, is enough to live out your life on." Proxmeyer smiled wistfully, putting the stub of his cigar back into his desk drawer now that it had gone cold.

"No one ever collected that reward," Shell said.

Proxmeyer glanced sharply at Shell. "No," he replied, "they didn't. Ten thousand dollars, as I say, was a hell of a lot of money, but it was nothing compared to what the kidnappers wanted. Old man Dormer got an unsigned letter demanding a half a million dollars in hard money—gold and silver—for the return of his son."

"He paid this?" Carmalita asked in astonishment.

"He paid it, but it was already too late. Cassius Dormer was found a week later, dead and dismembered. He likely had died the first night. The body had been long dead."

"There was no trace of the kidnappers?" Shell asked.

"None. And there was a fifty thousand reward by then.

Men from thirty states were tramping around that desert running into each other. Couple of men were shot by accident. But the gang had plain vanished. So had th gold.''

"Rough way to act as someone's benefactor," Shel said, his voice oddly tight. Proxmeyer blinked at him an Carmalita stared.

"Now, Mister Hurt, suppose you tell me what yo know about this."

"Nothing," Shelter said honestly. "Only what yo told me."

"And that name just sort of drifted into the conversa tion out of thin air."

"Something like that."

This bothered Shelter, bothered him a lot. Some year back a man named Cassius Dormer had been kidnappe and murdered. A ransom of half a million dollars ha been taken. At the citadel they claimed a man name Dormer had been their "Benefactor". They lived ou there away from all eyes, their horde of gold hidde away. Five thousand dollars had been buried with tha "saint" Shelter had found. What exactly was five thou sand times the hundred or so people who lived in the cita del? Even with Shelter's somewhat weak math it cam out to half a million dollars in hard money.

That pegged it. Kamolay, whatever his original nam had been, was once the leader of an outlaw gang. Fo whatever reason they had taken refuge in that mesa, tak ing others along with them, cutting them in on the ran som, money which was never to be spent.

It was vague and confusing, but some part of it had t be true.

So what did he have now? One of them from th

citadel—Brother Thomas—wanted to take some of that gold and spend it instead of burying it. He had contacted Dantworth, or Dabb, for the job. Knowing Dabb as Shell did, he doubted Brother Thomas would ever see a dollar of that money. He would be buried himself. Without any gold to keep him company in the grave.

Shell walked out into the street with Carmalita. He was silent as he guided her toward the buggy.

What exactly was his responsibility? One gang of killers riding out there to kill another gang of thieves and murderers. Damn right!

For the leader of that gang was Horatio Dabb, and he must be put to rest before he killed anyone again. As for the folks in the citadel, it was obvious that not all of them had been thieves. Something had happened to Kamolay, or perhaps he had been using them all for cover. But, recalling some of the faces, the quiet fortitude of those industrious people, he knew they had not all been criminals. And they—the innocents—were going to be in the way.

People like Freida.

His heart picked up a little as he thought of her. She was a confused, simple girl. Maybe somewhere deep inside she remembered the old Kamolay, for despite her belief, she hadn't been born in that citadel, she had been taken there and hidden away since childhood, a fragrant, beautiful flower flourishing in the darkness.

"What are you thinking of, Shelter Morgan?" Carmalita asked.

"What did you say?" Shell came suddenly alert.

"I asked what you were thinking of." They had halted beside the buggy and now Carmalita turned toward him, leaning against the wheel, smiling enigmatically.

139

"The name you used."

"Shelter Morgan?" She cocked her head and peered at him. "What else should I call you? It is your name, no?"

"Who told you."

"Told me?" She laughed out loud. "Why did someone have to tell me? I am stupid? A man comes to my house but he don't look at me, he looks through my husband's papers. He asks too many questions. He wears a gun like one who intends to use it. He kills one of my husband's pistoleros like swatting a fly. He comes off the desert, from nowhere and comes to our rancho. I know who you are, Mister Morgan. I have heard you described enough, heard you damned on my husband's lips."

"You must be crazy," Shelter growled.

"No, I don't think so. Not stupid and not crazy."

Shell helped her up onto the buggy seat then stepped up himself, sparing a quick look for the low hulking mesa which rested out on the desert.

"You will take the sheriff or other men with you when you go to kill him?" Carmalita asked. Shell was turning the buggy around. He shot a glance at Carmalita.

"Kill who?"

Carmalita laughed again, with some bitterness. "I have told you Carmalita is not stupid. I hear someone say 'half a million dollars' and I know my husband is involved. I see you and I know you are involved too. I know that my husband will kill you if he sees you. I know that you will kill him."

"Which would make you unhappy."

"Yes, a little," Carmalita said. They were out of town now, flying along the rutted road toward the Double D as the sun heeled over and began its downward descent. "I told you I did not want harm to come to my husband. He

140

gives me much, does much for my family. But he is also a bad man. Very bad, Mister . . . uh, Hurt. Sometimes he is so bad I hate him. He can be very cruel. So I am happy that he is gone much of the time. Maybe it would be good if he were always gone. I do not know.''

They drove in silence after that, Shell's eyes alert and probing. Just where in hell *was* Dabb? It had been hours since Dewey had met with Brother Thomas. Had that been their first meeting?—unlikely, Shell decided.

Thomas had known where he was going, and remembering the tone of their voices, the familiarity in them, he decided it had been the *last* meeting.

Dabb was ready to strike.

Likely they had just been waiting for Dabb to return from another piece of work, meaning of course, that Dabb was here now. At the rancho.

Shell felt his pulse rate increasing. It would be soon. Soon that he caught that bastard in his sights and finished what had begun so long ago along the Conasauga River in Georgia.

Shell saw the dust, saw the small dark figures and he swung the buggy violently to the side of the road. He whipped the big black horse mercilessly and it broke its gait, running headlong toward the dry, brushy wash to the west.

Carmalita held on for dear life, her eyes wide and questioning. But not frightened, never frightened. The buggy jolted to a stop among some long dead, gray willow brush and Shell leaped from the buggy, drawing his Colt.

It took them a while longer to crest the knoll, but soon they came around the bend. Carmalita was beside him and he pressed her to the ground with one arm while his right hand brought the Colt into position.

141

A dozen men, two dozen, riding slowly eastward passed and Shell watched them, his heart racing, his thumb hooked over the hammer of his .44.

He watched them file past, their horses' hoofs shuffling, raising dust. Twenty armed men, grim and determined.

Dabb!

He saw him suddenly, briefly, behind the column where Shelter couldn't get a clean shot—a shot that would have meant Shelter's own death, but one which would have been tempting.

Then they were gone, riding silently on, only the slowly settling dust marking their passage. Shell grimaced and shoved his Colt back into his holster.

Carmalita had rolled onto her back and now she lay there, looking up at him with shining black eyes. Her blouse had fallen open and Shelter had a view of those magnificent breasts full, upthrust, tempting.

Oddly he felt the urge to take her then and there and her widening eyes, her quickening breathing indicated that she was ready, wanting it.

"There's no time, Carmalita."

"I know this. But soon. You must come back and lay me down, Shelter Morgan."

He grinned, bent his head to hers and kissed her eager lips. Then he stood and tugged her to her feet. He stood a moment staring eastward, where the bandits had vanished. Then he lifted her onto the buggy step, clambered aboard himself and set off at a run toward the Double D.

Shell urged the horse on, guiding it down into the green valley. He didn't drive toward the main house, but swerved toward the bunkhouse, whipping through the yard in a cloud of dust, Carmalita holding on determinedly.

Teal, the cook, shouted something Shell didn't hear and shook his fist as Shelter halted beside the corral where his roan raised expectant eyes.

"Goodbye," Shell said.

"Goodbye." She touched his hand and smiled bittersweetly. *Via con Dios,* Mister Shelter Morgan." Slowly then she took the reins and turned the buggy, looking back over her shoulder only once.

Shell strode to the barn where his saddle was stored, shouldered it and walked back to the corral. He met a red-faced Buck Bascomb.

"Damnit, Hurt! What the hell are you up to? Where have you been anyway, out screwing the boss's wife?"

Shelter was tightening his cinches, ignoring Buck. "Can't do that?" he asked without looking back at the Double D foreman.

"No, by God!"

"Then I quit. So long, Buck." Shelter swung up into leather, nodded amiably and heeled the big roan forward, leaving Buck Bascomb to stand scratching his head in the sun-bright yard.

What now? Shelter rode the long-striding roan eastward, toward the desert flats. Logic told him he needed help and that the sheriff should be notified. A little reflection told him that he wasn't going to get any help from that quarter.

No it was up to Morgan, and him, alone. There was going to be a slaughter of innocents out at the citadel, and he alone could do something to stop it.

He was only afraid that it would be too damned little too late.

Or maybe not at all.

The three men on horseback came out of the draw, their guns blazing.

13.

They had been waiting. Dabb was no fool. Now they were coming, their guns blasting away the desert stillness. Shell palmed his Colt and fired back, seeing one man blown back off his horse.

Almost at the same moment he felt the roan buckle at the knees and start to somersault. Shell kicked out of the stirrups and leaped to one side, rolling as he hit the earth.

He came up on one knee, Colt ready as a second gunman—the one called Tabor—tried to run him down with his sorrel horse.

Shell fired into the chest of the sorrel and saw the horse cartwheel. Tabor's eyes were open wide, his mouth screaming as the horse flipped and Tabor was crushed beneath it.

That left one.

The bullets whined past Morgan and he flung himself

to the left, firing as he went. The bullet, a lucky one, tore into the outlaw's groin, ripping him open. He fell to the earth on his back and he lay there screaming with the pain, holding his crotch which was nothing but a red cavity.

"Just kill me!" the outlaw screamed. Blood leaked from his mouth as his head rolled from side to side. His glazed eyes found Morgan. "Do it, please!"

Shell stood over him and squeezed the trigger. The outlaw's scream fell away to silence.

Morgan walked to where the other dead lay. Tabor was staring without blinking at the fierce white sun, his spine snapped. The third gunman had a hole in his chest the size of Shell's fist.

He caught up the reins to one of the outlaw horses, a strapping buckskin, and stepped into leather. He glanced regretfully at the dead roan and then yanked the buckskin's head around, heeling it roughly, riding it out onto the broad and barren desert, his eyes lifting to the silent mesa beyond.

He rode rapidly, the horse laboring but in no danger of exhausting itself. It was still hot on the flats although the western sun was low, casting long crooked shadows before Morgan as he rode.

He checked the Winchester repeater which was in the outlaw's saddle boot and found it fully loaded, spanking new. Dabb's men apparently always had the best.

Just what he was going to do once he reached the mesa was something he hadn't yet determined. It was possible that he could still beat Dabb to the citadel, but not likely.

How would Dabb gain entrance? The stable door, no doubt. If Brother Thomas were to leave that open the outlaws could sweep into the interior of the citadel and strike

146

so quickly that no one could escape.

It would be the stable door. Hidden behind a screen of brush, plastered over to exactly duplicate the mesa walls it was impossible to detect unless it was revealed to any predator.

Well, it had been revealed, and that most predatory of men, the bastard Horatio Dabb was on his way.

So too was Shelter Morgan, and Morgan already knew that one of them would not live to see the morning sunrise.

He nudged the buckskin horse he rode into a canter and watched the broad expanse of red sand desert sweep past. Nothing seemed to live out there. Here and there ocotillo, flowering crimson at their tips, grew, and now and again Shell saw a clump of greasewood, a stray mesquite bush, but nothing seemed to crawl, to lope, to walk the desert. It was all illusion.

The Chiricahua owned this land and they were never far away. They were a wily people, a people given to sudden assault, sudden pursuit and slow, lingering deaths.

Shell urged the buckskin on, knowing now what he must do.

To try the stable entrance was suicide. Undoubtedly Dabb would post armed men there. It had to be from the top. Shell had to climb the mesa once more and enter the citadel through the graveyard. He had seen the stone moved once and he knew that he could move it again.

It would give him a small edge, the element of surprise. Then all he would have to do was to overwhelm two dozen or more men by himself, fighting his way through the long stone corridors of the citadel.

He smiled ruefully. "Nothing to it, Morgan," he said slowly.

He knew the chance he was taking, knew it was likely suicidal. But then, what chance did the people in the citadel have, gentle, unarmed people who would be chopped down before the guns of Dabb and his men?

"None at all," Shell told himself. The bulk of the mesa grew larger and Morgan swung the buckskin northward, his eyes sweeping the desert for signs of Dabb and his men. He saw nothing, but was not lulled into complacency. They could be gathering still in Delgado, or they could be already inside the citadel, already butchering the innocents.

Sunset was settling across the evening skies. Deep purple drapes were drawn across the land. Scarlet arrows pierced the violet-gray of the western clouds, sketching brief, vividly drawn images.

Shelter was in the shadow of the mesa, the buckskin tiring beneath him. He had to circle wide around the giant landform to find the canyon he knew too well. He rode the buckskin as far up the slanting canyon trail as possible. Then, reluctantly, he unsaddled, slipped the bit from the horse's mouth, slapped it on the flank and watched as it wandered in confusion back down the canyon.

Some Apache would be well-mounted tomorrow.

Shell took his bowie and slit the saddle blanket in his hand, cutting it into narrow strips. From these he fashioned a sling for the Winchester repeater. Then he began to climb.

He scrambled up the familiar yet alien trail as darkness settled across the empty land. Still he had heard no guns, no shrill cries of pain, and for a bare moment he harbored doubt.

Perhaps he had read this all wrong. Brother Thomas didn't necessarily have to have been giving away information. Dabb didn't necessarily have to have risen to the bait, to have decided on this night that he would kill all who stood between himself and a half million dollars in gold and silver.

No, and the sun didn't necessarily have to come up in the morning.

Shell had more than certain knowledge, he had that *feeling*. That sudden, gut-wrenching, physical knowledge that what he suspected was true.

It was a combat sense. Not something worked out within the mind, logically and coolly arrived at, but a knowledge beyond reason. It was true.

His senses jangled with the knowledge that Dabb would come on this night. His heart beat steadily, slowly, his every nerve ending was alert and anxious.

The man would be here.

Shell reached the caprock and wearily rose to stride across the flat pinnacle of the mesa. The shadows were deep beneath the cedars. The western sky was black with only a wisp of crimson to mark the sunset.

The tombstones were dark memorials to a dying race looming against the empty night sky.

Shell was among the ancient slabs, moving quickly toward the entrance to the citadel. He had nearly reached it when the first muted shot echoed up from the caverns below, a bellow rising from the bowels of the earth. The death-summons, the call to the final battle, Armageddon.

The slaughter had begun.

Morgan moved to the monument and pressed it as Freida had. Slowly it swung up on its axis, slowly the torchlit tunnel was revealed and Shelter Morgan, with a feeling akin to descending into hell, clambered into the maw.

Inside the tunnel the sound of gunshots were louder, but still distant, muffled, flat. Shelter heard voices, excited gabbling, somewhere below. He moved down the tunnel quickly, not expecting trouble this far away from the stable.

Torchlight flickered on the cavern walls. Shell's boot heels clicked on the stone floor. The shots and frightened voices from far below blended into an excited humming. It was like being inside a giant wasps' nest.

He found the council chamber and kicked the heavy door open. The room was empty. Kamolay was not there although a half-eaten plate of vegetables sat at the head of the table.

Shell hurried out of the massive room and jogged toward Freida's room, hoping against hope that she was there. If she was, Shelter planned on taking her back to the tunnel entrance, hiding her on the caprock if he had to tie her to keep her up there.

Her room too was empty.

Cursing, Shelter turned and started down the tunnels. The shots had all but died away now although all sorts of strange, unidentifiable sounds filtered up through the vast cavern, muted by the distances, echoing and re-echoing through the honeycomb.

He found a group of people at the garden ledge, looking helplessly out at the dark night then back at the tunnel mouth.

"You've got to go up to the top of the mesa," Shell told them.

"What has happened?" a blank-faced woman asked tremulously.

"Listen, there are enemies in the citadel. You've got to go up and exit through the graveyard."

"What has happened?" a thin, frail-appearing man asked and Shelter gnashed his teeth in frustration.

He tried another way: "Kamolay has directed you to leave this place for now. Go out onto the mesa."

That got them moving. They looked at each other for a minute, then with some murmuring, a lot of hand-wringing and some lamentations, they started up the tunnel.

"Wait," Shelter said, "where is Freida?"

"We have not seen her, stranger Morgan."

Shell was already up and moving, rifle in his hands, ducking low to clear the low ceiling of a feeder tunnel. He rounded a bend in the shaft and came face to face with an outlaw.

The man's gun was still smoking and behind him Shell saw a crumpled white figure lying on the gray stone floor. Shelter didn't even think about it. He jabbed out with his Winchester, squeezing the trigger as the muzzle touched the outlaw's face.

The headless outlaw staggered back to flop to the floor beside his victim.

Shell leaped over the bodies and ran on, an anger building in him.

These bastards had broken in here to steal that money. If they had to kill a hundred people to make sure they got away with it, then they would.

It made no difference to them that the worst of these people was better than all of the outlaws combined, that they were defenseless, that they had the same right to a long happy existence as they did. That, by God, they were men and women! Not hogs to be slaughtered.

Shell halted and pressed himself against the wall of the tunnel, hearing footsteps.

151

These footsteps weren't being made by people who lived in the citadel. They wore hard heeled boots. Shell shifted his rifle to his left hand and drew his Colt, holding it up, the barrel beside his ear.

When they came around the corner Shell stepped out and started firing. There were two of them. The first was blown back in a crumpled heap. The second man got a shot off, but the bullet flew wide, singing off the stony cavern walls.

Shell didn't miss. He got him dead center, a gut shot and the outlaw fell, clutching his belly, writhing in pain. Morgan couldn't drum up any sympathy for him. Shell picked up his guns, tucking the pistol into his own belt, tossing the rifle away.

The outlaw with a perspiration-glossed face looked up at Shell, his lips twisting into a silent curse. Shell simply stepped over him and continued.

The torches were out. That was the first thing he noticed on rounding the bend in the tunnel. The blackness was overwhelming and Shell was forced to inch his way along the passageway, feeling the wall for direction.

He was bathed in darkness, still hearing the distant sounds of panic and pain. His shirt was pasted to his body with sweat. The Colt in his hand was cool, cocked and ready.

He nearly stumbled over her.

The woman screamed and Shell bent down, touching her head. "Be quiet, woman, I'm here to help you."

"Shelter."

It was Freida. She stood and melted into his arms and he held her tightly in the complete darkness of the citadel. He kissed her forehead lightly and felt her quivering in his arms.

"Where are they?"

"They came in through the stable. We didn't have any warning. They're killing everyone!"

"All right. Calm down now. Where are they now?"

"The vault," was all she could say.

"What vault, Freida?" Suddenly he knew. "The bricks. The brick wall. Is that it? Behind that is where the gold is kept?"

"Yes. It is there." She shivered, a small, defenseless thing, a creature not made for this world, or any other.

"All right. I'll go on down. I want you to go up to the top of the mesa and hide. Hide anywhere, but get out of the citadel."

"No." He felt Freida stiffen in his arms and draw away. "I will go with thee. I must know that Kamolay is uninjured."

"It's not safe, Freida. You're not helping any-thing . . ."

Shell fell silent. He could see the approaching torch-light, hear the bootheels on the cavern floor despite the fact that someone was making every effort to move cau-tiously.

"This way," Freida whispered and Shelter held onto her robe, following. She had spent the bulk of her life in this strange subterranean world, and Freida moved along as if she had cat's eyes or the senses of a bat. Shell had to tug at her robe to slow her down.

"Duck," she whispered and Shelter did so. Freida led him forward into another tunnel, low, not quite dark. Looking up he saw starlight falling through a gaping cleft in the caprock far above them.

"No one comes this way," Freida said. "It is a dan-gerous tunnel. We abandoned it long ago. Look out now."

No sooner had she said that then Shell, looking down, saw the yawning maw of a deep pit where the floor had fallen away. Parts of the wall had caved in as well. Tunneling had weakened the inherent strength of the mesa. Freida hoisted her robe, backed up three paces and ran forward, leaping the twelve-foot chasm. Shell followed her, landing awkwardly on the far side.

"Where does this lead?" he asked Freida.

"Where? Why to the vault of course. Is that not where thou wished to go?"

"Yes. It is there that I wished to go," Shelter said grimly. There where the gold was stored, the ransom from a decade-old crime, there where Kamolay presumably was to be found. There, where the bastard Horatio Dabb would die.

14.

They rushed on through the broken, disused tunnel, at times having to scramble over huge piles of rubble which had sloughed off from the crumbling walls. Shell, seeing all of this, again realized that the citadel was in real danger of collapsing one day. The lava had left a honeycombed structure which eons of water had scoured, which the saints, in their attempts to make a home out of this hiding place had chipped away at. The mesa was a huge chocolate cake with the guts torn out of it.

Shots again! Shelter halted drawing Freida to him. They could see nothing, but the guns were near at hand. More were dying. More paying the price for the bright, deadly yellow metal.

"Where are we?" Shelter asked.

"It's not far. One more bend. We will emerge on a edge above the store room. From there we shall be able

155

to look down on the vault.

Shell nodded and whispered, "Lead on." Just what he was going to do against twenty men he hadn't yet figured out. It didn't matter. Dabb was going to die, and if Shelter had to lock his hands around Dabb's throat and be dragged down into hell with him, then that was the way it would be.

They didn't make the next bend.

They came out of the darkness. Thirteen men. Kamolay and behind him the twelve "men of misery". Shelter by instinct raised his pistol.

There was enough starlight behind them, enough torchlight filtering through from before them for Shelter to make out Kamolay's face, saving his life. The old man looked as old as the mesa itself now. He was beaten. His mouth hung down at the corners as if great weights had been tied on. He barely responded to Shell's sudden appearance.

"Freida," the old man said, "you should have run away. You should not have come back here."

"I could not run away while you were in danger, Father," she said.

"You are too loving, Freida." The old man wrapped his arms around her. "Too good for such as me." He paused, wiping back the hair which had fallen into her eyes. "I tried to do what was right. I tried to do what was best for you. I just didn't know . . . my sins have returned to me."

"Funny, isn't it," Morgan said. "You can't seem to outrun your crimes." He was thinking of Dabb as well but Kamolay got his meaning.

"You know."

"Sure."

156

"You are a lawman?" Kamolay asked.

"No. It just happened to come out. But then it would have sooner or later."

"What are you talking about?" Freida asked, her eyes shifting from Shell to her father and back again.

"I did a terrible thing in the pagan land," Kamolay said. "Most terrible."

"Father?"

Freida touched his arm. The old man's head was bowed. There was just enough light to see the tear streaking his cheek. "I tried to atone. We all did." He spread his arms, looking at the men of misery.

"I don't understand." Freida looked at Morgan, "Won't you tell me what happened?"

Shelter looked at Kamolay who slowly nodded, and Shell told her.

"A long while back a man named Cassius Dormer was kidnapped by a gang of thugs. They demanded a huge ransom in gold and silver, and it was paid. But the outlaws never intended to let Dormer live. He could identify them. They killed him brutally, making off with the ransom.

"Something happened. I don't know what. The guilt eroded the hardcases' souls. Maybe they saw a flaming star in the sky one night. Maybe they just couldn't look at the gold without seeing blood, the horror on a dying man's face.

"The leader of this gang took an oath—he had them all take it—they would never harm any living thing again. They would never spend a dollar of that money on themselves or worldly pleasures. It was filthy, and they were sinners.

"The leader of the gang had once been a prospector.

He had prowled most of New Mexico Territory and something caused him to recall a hollowed out mesa he had once explored. It was a place where they could be secure from the eyes of the law, a place where they could establish a colony and teach their followers that there was evil outside of this place, that gold was evil, worthless, that to harm anyone was despicable. That love alone mattered, that we are here to help one another, to go gently through this existence . . . am I saying this all right, Kamolay?''

"It is right."

"The outlaw, you see, had a little girl, and he was living in dread that she would grow up to discover he was a murdering thief. I don't know what all went on in the background. What happened to the wife of this man, what finally decided him—and the others.

"I do know they finally did come to this sanctuary, this citadel and there they planned to live out their lives atoning for the wrong they had done. Unfortunately one of their acolytes, a store keeper, was a man who himself felt the gold lust, and he fell in with evil men who came to the citadel to destroy it and all of the reformed outlaw's hopes.''

"It was Brother Thomas?'' Freida said. But her eyes were on her father, her other question unspoken.

The shots erupted close at hand, closing out any further discussion. Shell turned to the hooded men.

"They're going to be slaughtered, every one of them.''

"And there is nothing to be done about it.''

"Balls!'' Shell said angrily.

"We have taken an oath . . .''

"Yes, I know that. Men of misery. Reformed outlaws.

158

Great. You took an oath because you realized that what you were doing was wrong. Well, by God, you tell me what is worse than letting these innocent people be slaughtered like sheep!''

"I swore never again to pick up a gun," one of the hooded men said. Shell suddenly knew this man. The thin light caught his face in profile and Shell knew him.

"Clay Dawson!"

"I am Brother Michael."

"Fine. You used to be Clay Dawson, however. I met you sort of casually once, down in Alabama. You had a handful of the bank's money and a fistful of Colt Dragoon in the other hand.''

That wasn't the first or the last robbery Clay Dawson had pulled off. He had flourished throughout the war and then when reconstruction came in, he had become a sort of folk hero robbing the Yankee-held banks, the carpet-baggers' homes.

He had drifted west, been shot and killed, some said, but here he stood, a man in a cowled robe, sadly shaking his head.

"There was a man called Clay Dawson, but he is now dead. I am Brother Michael and I am a man of misery, weighed down with sorrow for the world of pain.''

Shell now stepped nearer to another "man of misery", and slipping back the cowl from the man's head he disclosed "Judge" Blount, a man wanted in Texas and Arkansas, the Indian Nation and most of the West for capital crimes including the murder of six law officers who had come looking for him in a Cabin Creek hideout.

"Damn me," Shell said. "Blount."

"I am Brother James, a man of misery," said Blount and Shelter grimaced. Judge Blount went through the

159

same confession Clay Dawson had. Whatever Kamolay had experienced, he had obviously brought to these members of what had to have been a fearsome gang.

To a man they had gotten religion, of the strange sort Kamolay preached. Shelter moved among them, pulling back their cowls, recognizing Kid Abilene, older, grayer, Tom Short, Mad Jack Rivers.

The rest he did not know, but they were all tough, competent-looking men. He faced them as the gunshots again rang out from below.

"You men did right," Shell said. "You were evil."

"Amen," they responded.

"All right. You put aside your guns and tried to reform. You did what had to be done."

"Amen."

"But, by God, it's time to strap guns back on."

"To take a life is obscene," Judge Blount said. "It is an abomination."

"Yes," Shell agreed. "But what is it to stand by and let innocent people be slaughtered when you have the skills and the means to stop it!"

"I vowed to never again kill," Clay Dawson said.

"I can respect that," Shell said, speaking rapidly now. "I'd like to be able to take the same vow myself. But the thing is you took that vow because you knew that what you had been doing was *wrong*. I'm telling you, Clay, Brother Michael, it's not wrong to protect the innocents from a man like Horatio Dabb. It's *wrong* to let the innocent be hurt."

Brother Michael, once the most feared gunfighter in the South stood, shaking his head slowly, looking to Kamolay for help.

"It is always wrong to kill," Kamolay said finally.

"But what can be more wrong than to avoid killing evil so that evil may survive to destroy innocence?"

"The oath . . ." A scream from below broke into the question and Kamolay, reverting to some harder personality swore:

"Damn the oath, Clay! They're shooting our people to death!"

"We've got no weapons," Clay Dawson said and Shelter tossed him one of his pistols. Dawson caught it deftly and with a sharp glance, one which was near relief, he spun the cylinder, checking the loads.

"Judge?"

Blount looked to Shell and Morgan handed him the Winchester. Solemnly he sook his head, "All right," Blount said. "May I be damned, I'm ready to take it to them."

"There's a man back up the tunnel," Morgan said. "He dropped a Winchester. If one of you wants to scoot back up and collect it, it would help."

Someone did. "The rest of you will have to wait for a time," Shell said. "When there's a chance, grab a weapon. These bastards have got to be driven out of here. You're not fighting for the gold; you're fighting for the people. Friends, good men and women."

Shell slipped his bowie from his sheath and gave it to Kamolay who took it, his grim mouth carved into a deep frown. Freida stood by, staring at Shell.

"You're telling them to kill! You're ruining it all. You are destroying peace!"

"Maybe." Morgan turned his eyes away. He nodded to Clay Dawson, "Let's go, Brother Michael. There's some holy wars need fighting."

The three armed men, followed by Kamolay who had

161

only a knife, and Freida who was numbed by the events, crept out onto the ledge which overlooked the walled-up vault where half a million dollars in gold and silver lay.

Creeping to the edge Shelter could look down upon the bricked in "vault" of the citadel where the gold lay concealed.

He could also see Dabb.

It took a moment before Shelter realized what was going on. Then he caught on. Of course—Thomas would have told them all about it. Dabb had come prepared.

The keg of black powder rested at the base of the brick wall and the fuse hissed and sparkled as Dabb touched a match to it. Five or six men stood beside him, watching. Beyond them Shelter could make out light which had to be coming up from the stable. There were three robed figures crumpled on the floor.

"Dabb!" Shell swung the muzzle of his Colt up and Dabb reacted. Instead of turning, looking up to the ledge to see who was calling him, he flung himself violently to one side, throwing himself out of Shelter's line of sight.

"Open up," Shell shouted and the robed men of misery, the most skilled gunmen of their time did so. Shelter saw Clay Dawson take down one outlaw, switch his sights and smoothly kill another.

Freida screamed. The guns roared and acrid smoke boiled up toward the ceiling of the cavern. Shell popped a shot off at a fleeing bandit, saw him fold up and skid on his face. Judge Blount had taken another outlaw, but more of Dabb's men were coming on the run.

"They're coming up from the stable," Blount shouted.

"Get the hell out of here!" Morgan said, leaping to his feet. Blount looked at him with puzzlement. The blank, distracted look was gone from his face. The last few minutes had molded the gunman's face into sharp relief. There was a hungry look in his eye. His lips were compressed tightly.

"Why back up now?"

"The powder," Shelter called. Then he ducked low and re-entered the disused tunnel where Kamolay already stood, shaking, his mouth open gasping for air.

The keg of powder went off just as Judge Blount reached the tunnel. There was a white flash behind him, a jutting red tongue of flame and Blount was blown forward, his arms grasping at the air, searching for handholds which didn't exist.

The tunnel flooring shook and rubble fell from the walls. Billowing smoke rolled up from the vault room below and Shelter had to fall back, his arm over his face, Freida clinging to his belt.

He nearly tripped over Kamolay who had gone down as a half ton of rubble slid off the wall of the tunnel, sweeping his feet from under him.

"I am all right," Kamolay said. "Go on."

Shelter ignored him and began digging Kamolay out of the rubble. Stone was falling in huge sections from the tunnel ceiling now and Shelter had to leap back, pulling Kamolay with him as tons of stone and earth collapsed, filling the tunnel with swirling dust.

"That charge—" Judge Blount panted. "Bastard used way too much powder."

Blount, who had blown a safe or two in his time, was right. The cavern still echoed, still vibrated. Stone still fell from the weakened walls and ceiling.

"Let's get the hell out of here," Shell said. He was practically holding Kamolay upright. "Which way?"

"What?" Kamolay's eyes were unfocused. He was

163

limp in Shell's hands.

"Which way!"

"Stranger Morgan!" Freida pointed at the wall to the south which even in that poor light they could see slowly separating, shuddering as the weight of the mesa, weakened by the explosion, slowly sagged downward.

"Which way out!" Shell demanded.

"Here," Freida said quickly. "Follow me."

That was easier said than done. There were no torches in this tunnel and the smoke was cutting out the light from below. A bit of starlight fell through the open ceiling of the decayed tunnel, but it was barely enough to even give a sense of direction. Shell could make out the white-robed girl only intermittently as she led the way up the tunnel.

"Sing out when you reach that shaft!" Morgan called. Kamolay was still on his arm, reeling as Shell led him up the long, sloping shaft.

"Who's that!"

They heard Freida ask that and their guns came up instinctively. A voice answered hurriedly.

"It's me, Sister."

A man appeared—one of those Shelter had sent back up to look for another weapon. He emerged from the dark haze to stand before them.

"It's no good," he told them.

"What's no good, Curly?" Judge Blount asked. Suddenly no one was Brother-such-and-such. They were Curly and Clay, Judge again.

"It's all coming down up there . . ." Curly panted. "The library roof fell in. The council tunnel is collapsed. You can't get through up there. The whole damn mesa's coming apart."

164

15.

No one spoke for a long minute. Shelter heard a chattering sound, realized it was Freida's teeth clacking together in fear and slowly cursed. The walls around him creaked and groaned. There wasn't any time for long decision making.

"There's no way out?"

"Not unless you want to jump a hundred feet," Curly said. "And believe me I thought about it . . . when this goes . . ." he looked up and shuddered.

"What do we do now, Morgan?"

"There's no choice—we take it to them"

"Back down?" Freida asked in despair.

"It's the only way."

"There's twenty armed men down there."

"It's that or sit and wait to run out of air, wait for the mesa to crush us. What do you want to do, Judge?"

"Hell," he muttered, "let's take it to them."

He had no more enthusiasm for it than Shelter did. But they followed him back through the littered corridor toward the vault where the smoke still hung in a thick pall.

They burst onto the ledge, guns blazing. Dabb's men had been waiting. A bullet ripped into Curly's shoulder and he screamed, his rifle clattering to the stone floor of the ledge. Shelter, going to a knee, cut loose with his Colt, emptying it in the direction of the outlaws below him.

He shoveled fresh loads into the cylinder as Judge Blount's rifle racketed beside his ear. Shell saw a man go down behind the pile of blackened, broken bricks. There was another flurry of shots from below and then the Dabb men started pulling back, some of them dragging bags of gold. Shelter stood, fired, saw a man sag over his money bag and lay still. Then he leaped the twenty feet to the ground and called back over his shoulder, "Let's go. Let's get the hell out of here!"

Dawson came flying through the air, his white robe billowing out, his rifle firmly in his grip. He landed beside Shell and got to his feet in time to trigger off a shot at a Dabb man who had for some reason, perhaps greed—stayed behind in the vault to bring out a last bag of gold. It cost him his life.

"I can't jump!" Freida was wailing from above.

"Give her the count of three, Judge, then throw her," Shell ordered.

At that Freida closed her eyes and jumped, Dawson and Shell managing to break her fall. Kamolay was next. He was moving woodenly, his eyes blank. His world was falling apart.

"My sins have been visited upon me," he kept mut-

166

tering.

Judge Blount was down now and they made their way toward the stables, moving single file, keeping close to the walls where still torches burned despite the shock wave from the explosion.

Rounding the corner Shell saw a muzzle flash. The bullet whined off the stone wall as he drew back, ducked and fired his own gun. A cry of agony filled the cavern and they went forward again.

"Damn me. It's coming down," Judge Blount said, and he seemed to be right. The walls shook, the floor underfoot rumbled and swayed. Shell looked upward, concern lining his face.

Now he could see a patch of sky. The stable door. Shell rushed on, eyes darting into every shadowed corner of the great cavern. He found the man he had shot, dead. There was no one else.

A few gold pieces were scattered across the floor of the stable, gleaming dully in the starlight which shone through the open door.

There was nothing moving beyond that door, nothing but the slowly sifting dust of Dabb's horses.

"Morgan!" Judge Blount's voice was anxious. "We've got to get moving."

"All right." Shell found half a dozen horses still in their stalls. Dabb had had no need for them and either hadn't wanted to take the time or hadn't thought of turning them out. "Get them outside. Outside. We'll saddle up out there."

Shelter grabbed the mane of a big, loose jointed blue roan and jogged with it toward the stable entrance. Freida stood unmoving in the center of the dark, dusty stable.

"Get moving! Freida!"

167

"How can I leave the citadel? What will happen to me once I go into the pagan lands?" She turned in a slow circle. Shell, giving his horse over to Clay Dawson, returned, flipped Freida over his shoulder and dashed for the door, expecting the roof to come in at any moment.

Remarkably it still held up. The mesa was like a rotted, hollow tree, awaiting only the casual wind to topple it. When it went it would be like the report of ten thousand cannon. Morgan knew he didn't want to be anywhere around when it happened.

"Freida?" She was standing beside the bay horse which Blount had saddled for her, simply staring while Kamolay went on about his sins visiting him.

"I've never ridden a horse."

"You'll start learning now. Kamolay—stop that howling," Shelter said harshly. "Get up on that damned horse and take your daughter with you. Ride into Delgado and find someplace to hole up. Anyplace, maybe they've a church in town, I didn't notice."

"But you . . ." Freida said. The night breeze was twisting through her dark hair. Her eyes were wide and frightened. A child's eyes.

"I'm going after the man."

"Don't!" Kamolay shouted. "Let them have the gold. What do I care about that! It's blood money, let the man have it."

"And get away with killing your people."

"Vengeance is mine saith . . ."

"No. It's mine," Shelter said. "And I'm bringing that vengeance home."

"I'd be pleased to ride with you, Morgan," Judge Blount said. "Me and Clay."

"I'd be pleased to have you," Morgan said. He

glanced back across his shoulder. "Now let's get the hell out of here."

"There are still people back there," Kamolay said, his voice weak.

"They've either gotten to safety or they won't make it," Shell answered. He swung into the saddle, feeling as bad as Kamolay did, not daring to let it show. What Morgan said was true enough; the thing was, not many of them could have made it out.

"I brought them here," Kamolay said. "I wanted to save them . . ." he bowed his head and began to sob. It was a heartbreaking sound in the night.

"What's that?" Judge Blount asked. The ground beneath them began to rumble and shift. All eyes lifted toward the mesa.

"Get away from it!" Clay Dawson shouted and they heeled their horses, making their run. They were only half a mile away when the mesa finally gave way. They saw the caprock sag, felt the rolling of the earth beneath them. Then it all went, the sound like an armory exploding. Shell was nearly thrown from his horse's back as the mesa crumbled, and the ground shook. The horses whinnied, dancing in terror as the tremors jerked away at the earth beneath their hoofs.

It was there and then it was not. There was only a pile of rubble, massive and confused, a dust cloud rising a mile into the starlit night, the residual groaning of settling rock as the citadel died.

It would remain there forever, the gentle winds, the sand, the rain smoothing the jagged contours. In time, in hundreds of years no one would know what had happened. There would be nothing of the citadel and one man's dream of a good world but a low mound sitting

169

alone on a bleak and empty desert.

"Let's go," Shell said, breaking the spell. *How many more, Dabb?* How many more would have to die because of this man's greed, his blood lust?

Not one if Morgan could help it. Or maybe just one more—Shelter Morgan himself.

They parted from Kamolay and Freida a mile from town. Kamolay was in a daze. Shelter doubted if he knew where he was.

"You take care of him Freida. If you can't find a place to stay, try talking to the sheriff, maybe he can help you out."

"He can't be seen by no lawman," Clay Dawson said. Dawson sat there in his robe, the hood thrown back. He looked tough and competent. The years spent in the citadel seemed to have been washed away on this single night.

"No one would recognize him now, Clay," Morgan said.

"Maybe so, Maybe no. That reward might still be good."

"I won't go to the sheriff," Freida said, settling it.

"All right. Take care of him, Freida. Now he needs you."

"Yes. Now he does," she repeated. The three men watched as Freida led her father toward the distant, dim lights of Delgado, and when there was nothing more to be seen of the white-clad figures Shelter turned in his saddle and said:

"I'm going after him now. You boys don't have to get mixed up in this."

"We're going, I told you."

"Maybe it's a special kind of atonement," Clay Dawson said. "Like Kamolay was always talking about—atonement."

"They killed them people, Shelter. They were people we lived with and knew." Judge Blount glanced at Dawson and said, "We're comin' in, and those boys better be ready. There's nothin' more dangerous than a man who doesn't care if he lives or dies, and Morgan, just now I don't care one way or the other as long as I see some of them go first."

Nothing more was said. Shell nudged his blue roan into motion and they rode westward toward the Double D as the low crescent moon, shining through the haze the crumbling mesa had spread against the night sky, silvered the sand before them.

It was shortly before midnight when they came upon the Dabb house. It was late, but there was plenty of activity in the house and around it.

There were two dozen horses in the yard and the house was ablaze with light. Shelter, flanked by Clay Dawson and Judge Blount sat his horse on the low hillrise and studied first the house then the surrounding country.

"He'll have plenty of sentries out," Dawson said. "There," he pointed, "and there, along the river where the willows are so thick."

"Probably on the roof of the house as well," Judge chipped in. Shell nodded.

"You're right. We ride in there like this, we're asking to be chopped down. And that won't do." Not until Dabb himself went down.

"Any ideas?"

"Just one," Morgan said. "There's a ravine on the far side of the house. I scouted it one day. It's possible to slip to within a hundred feet or so of the house without being seen."

"A hundred feet," Dawson mused.

"From then on it's rolling dice."

"Get us within a hundred feet," Judge Blount said, "and from there on in I'll take my chances."

Shell grinned in the darkness. These men had come to fight. Well, they could have all they wanted of it. Tonight this little valley would be stained red.

"Let's go," Morgan said. "We've got to circle back a ways. There's a trail a mile or so upriver."

They moved silently through the night. Dawson and Blount had shed their white robes. They were just too visible at night. Each wore a sort of loincloth wrapped around him, giving them the appearance of a pair of Indian fakirs. If either was embarrassed they gave no indication of it.

They had come to fight. Their thoughts were on death, not on their bizarre dress.

The bunkhouse was still and silent. The weary cowhands were unaware of any of the activity down below. That was the way Dabb had wanted it, the reason for this set-up. Shelter brought the two former outlaws up behind the bunkhouse, keeping to the shadows cast by the old sycamore.

Shell nodded and they stepped from their horses, dropping the reins. Shelter took a deep breath, let his eyes search the bunkhouse, the night shadows, the Dabb house below which blazed with light. They would be dividing the gold up now, perhaps having a round of drinks to celebrate. Dabb would be flushed with success, smiling with enjoyment. Shelter meant to wipe that smile right off his face.

Gesturing, Shell led the others toward the ravine he

had scouted earlier in the week. The shadows were deep in the canyon, the night still, but they moved cautiously, guns ready. It was no time to take chances.

In ten minutes they were at the mouth of the ravine, pressed against the ground, studying the back of the Dabb house. A sentry strode past, extra alert on this night. Shell recognized him as he passed through the wedge of light which bled out through the kitchen window. It was Daltry.

They held their position for a long while, trying to get the feel of the guards' movements, measuring the time a man would have to bolt toward the house as the guard rounded the far corner.

Dawson jabbed a finger into Shell's side and pointed to the roof of the big house. Shelter saw a vague silhouette shift, heard a small scraping noise. They were on the roof too.

On the roof, in the willows along the river, on every good observation point surrounding the house. And inside dozens more guns with hard men behind them. It was damned near an impossible situation and each of them knew it.

Shelter's voice was gravelly, his eyes narrowed, his muscles tense. He glanced at Judge Blount.

''Let's go on in.''

Maybe it was madness. Walking into hell to spit in the devil's eye, but it had to be done. There was no way of holding back Clay Dawson and Judge Blount anyway. It was as they said—they didn't give a damn if they lived or died.

Shell did. There was too much to be done yet, too many others who had begun their murderous careers that night along the Conasauga and Morgan meant to live long enough to pay each of them back.

Morgan went first. As Daltry rounded the corner of the house, Shell dashed toward the kitchen door. He hit the door at a full run, banging into it with his shoulder. It crashed open.

Shell crouched, swinging his Colt up. Amazingly the kitchen was empty, and crossing to the interior door, standing beside it, Shell heard no approaching footsteps. This was an opportunity he hadn't counted on, perhaps an opportunity to even things up a little.

He dashed back across the room, waved an arm at Judge and Clay, holding them back. Then he closed the door and crossed to the huge fireplace.

He searched for and found the flue, closed it and working hurriedly, prodded the fire to life, stacking a huge quantity of wood on top of the growing flames.

Already the smoke was rolling into the kitchen, and Shelter, satisfied, returned to the outside door.

He peered out and withdrew immediately. Daltry was within fifteen feet of the kitchen door. He heard the outlaw call softly:

"Juan?"

"*Si,*" Shelter answered just as softly.

"What in hell. . ." Daltry's puzzled voice fell away into a string of low curses. Shell saw the knob turn on the door, heard Daltry mutter, "What the hell," again as he saw the smoke-clogged kitchen.

Daltry stepped in and Shelter moved. He crooked his arm around Daltry's throat and drove up viciously with the big bowie. Daltry wriggled in his arms and then slumped to the floor, dead before he hit it.

Morgan slipped Daltry's Colt from his holster and tucked it behind his belt. Then, blowing out the lantern which hung beside the door, he stepped out into the shadowed yard. He pressed himself to the wall, letting his eyes adjust again to the darkness. When he could make out Dawson and Blount, he gestured, summoning them.

The two outlaws, running in a crouch, crossed the yard and . . . joined Shelter at the wall. The smoke was beginning to seep out from beneath the kitchen door, Shelter noted with satisfaction.

"Where?" Judge hissed.

Shelter pointed up and Judge saw the overhanging balcony above them. He nodded, shoved his pistol behind the waistband of his loincloth and interlocked his cupped hands.

Shell put a boot in the hands and was lifted toward the balcony railing. He swung himself up and over the wrought iron rail and glanced back, seeing Judge hoist Clay Dawson.

Shell caught Dawson's wrists and pulled him up beside him. Judge fell back into the shadows as Shelter tested the door and Dawson stood watch.

The door was locked, but it wasn't much of a door, only a light frame and two small glass panels. Shelter tapped the glass out with his Colt, the tinkling sound loud in the silent night. Then, finding the inside lock, he pushed the door open and he was in the house.

He and Clay Dawson were in an upstairs bedroom, guns in hand. The small sound from the bed announced the fact that they weren't alone.

Shell stepped to the bed and threw aside the covers. It was a delightful sight.

"Carmalita."

"I knew you would come back for me," she said drolly. She caught sight of the other man in her room and she pulled a sheet up to cover her breasts. "What is this?" Her eyes flashed from the open door to Shelter. "Is that smoke I smell?"

"It is. Carmalita, you've got to get out of here." Shell spoke rapidly, his voice an urgent whisper. She started to argue and Shelter held his breath. What did he really know about this woman except that she was breathtakingly beautiful, passionate and reckless. The chips were down now. Would she scream a warning? Her husband's money meant much to her. More than this wandering, tall man's loving? Shell stood poised, ready to crack her skull with the Colt if need be.

It wasn't necessary. Carmalita said, "Throw me that wrapper. I will go."

She slipped the wrapper on hurriedly while Shell paced the room. When she was ready he stepped out onto the balcony and looked quickly around. Then Carmalita was over the railing, Shell holding her wrists.

"Goodbye, Mister Morgan. I liked you very much."

Shell let her drop to the ground and scurry away before he turned back to Dawson, nodding.

"Let's take it to them, Clay. Let's give these boys a little taste of hell."

16.

Shelter opened the door onto the upstairs landing. There was no one there. The voices, the light came from below, and peering around the corner Shelter saw them sitting at the enormous, oval-shaped table in Dabb's dining room.

The center of the table was heaped with gold and silver, the gold in neat stacks now, the silver, being secondary, shoved aside in piles. They had crystal goblets filled with amber liquor and plates of cold beef before them—a hearty meal after a hard night's work. Shelter's throat was choked down with anger. His lips formed a snarling scowl. He looked at Clay Dawson who stood in that half-light, wearing only the loincloth he had worn beneath his robe, holding that big Colt beside his hip, looking deadly and savage.

Shelter nodded.

"Dabb!" Shelter hollered and before any of them could finish turning in their chairs to look up to the landing, Shelter opened up.

He saw Dabb spun around in his chair, saw the chair go over, saw Dabb scramble away on hands and knees. Shelter switched his sights to Dewey who was rising, slapping for his pistol. He had actually gotten it out of his holster before Shell's second bullet caught the redhead in the throat and he was blown back across the table, spilling blood across the gold which was knocked everywhere.

"Smoke! Damnit, they've fired the house!" someone shouted in sudden panic. Those were the last words that outlaw was ever to speak. Clay Dawson, firing coolly, shot him through the chest and the man went down, lurching into a cabinet filled with fine china and crystal.

The table had been upturned and the outlaws were firing from behind it, bullets singing through the big house, thudding into the wall at Shelter's back.

He could hear them screaming at each other:

"Out the back!"

"The house is on fire! The kitchen's filled with smoke!" It wasn't only the kitchen now, in fact. The smoke was creeping under the connecting door, adding to the lack of visibility as the battle continued.

Shelter emptied his Colt into the table, sat back behind the balustrade to reload and felt the impact of bullets in the heavy oak at his back. Dawson was still firing, calmly, efficiently. Another of the outlaws went down in a bloody heap.

Shelter snapped the loading gate shut, turned and began firing from behind the balustrade. He saw from the corner of his eyes the door to Dabb's office open, saw the blood soaked man in the tan coat crawl through and he jerked his muzzle to that side firing two shots rapidly. He missed. Dabb was into his office, badly wounded, but alive. In moment he would be out the window. Shelter swallowed a curse.

The smoke was boiling into the room below them now. The outlaws, coughing and choking fought back furiously. "Let's get the hell out of here!" someone yelled.

"And get shot down?"

"It's that or the smoke, damnit!"

There was a moment's hesitation and then the outlaw bolted for the front door, followed by three others. Shell's hammer dropped on an empty chamber and he cursed again.

They had nearly reached the front door when it burst open and an apparition in a loincloth, carrying a Winchester rifle blocked their path.

Judge Blount held the rifle at hip level and fired three times, working the lever like a machine. Two outlaws went down. The third, rolling aside, fired a shot which caught Blount in the face and he reeled back, dying in the doorway.

Clay Dawson screamed with anger. He leaped the balustrade and plummeted to the floor below, firing as he fell. He hit the floor, stepped to one side and walked in, emptying his Colt. Two more men went down never to rise again before Clay's pistol was empty and the two men left behind the table cut him down.

"Give it up!" Morgan yelled. "We've got the house surrounded."

They couldn't give it up. They would be hung by morning and so they fought back as the smoke rolled across the room as the balustrade around Shelter was splintered by the flying .44s.

Shell had to let them go. Loading his smoking pistol again he ran in a crouch back to the bedroom. Dabb would be making his run, and no matter what Shelter would not let him get away again.

He reached the balcony, swung over and dropped to the ground, seeing a dead guard below it. Judge Blount had done his work.

They opened up from the roof and Shelter flung himself to one side, the earth around him peppered with rifle fire. In the darkness he was able to crawl toward the cover of the trees beyond the yard as the searching fire probed the night.

Panting, Shell rolled to his belly and looked back at the house. He could make out the riflemen, in silhouette. More than that he could see that he had done his work too well. The kitchen had caught fire.

Flames curled up from the door and windows and licked at the eaves. If the riflemen didn't realize it yet, they soon would. All consideration for the fire was washed away by another, closer event.

He saw the shadowy figure hobble toward a horse and drag himself into the saddle, heard the drumming of hoofs and Shelter had time only to snap a wide shot off at the fleeing Horatio Dabb.

The report of his gun served to locate him once again for the men on the roof and their rifles spoke harshly, bullets cutting the foliage from the overhanging tree as Shell, pinned down, buried his face in his arms.

And all the time Dabb was making his getaway.

From the far side of the house, the front, there was a sudden, heavy exchange of gunfire and Shelter looked up, puzzled.

The rooftop snipers had switched around and now were

180

shooting into the front yard of the rancho. They stood, apparently giving it up as the flames crept up onto the roof, silhouetting them starkly. Shell saw one man dive for the edge of the roof, lose his grip and plummet screaming to the earth.

The horsemen rounded the corner of the casa, two men first, pursued by a dozen others. As Shelter watched one of the fleeing men went down. The other reined in sharply, throwing up his hands, preferring his chances with a judge.

Shelter could see the silver star by moonlight. It was pinned to the ragged vest of Sheriff Proxmeyer, and Shell went forward to meet him as the flames crackled around the big house, devouring it.

Now Shell, moving cautiously, hands over his head to avoid being shot by mistake, could see Buck Bascombe, Teal, Harmon, and other cowhands from the Double D sitting beside the sheriff.

"Halt."

"It's Shelter . . . It's Hurt, Sheriff!"

"That solves that," Proxmeyer said as Morgan went nearer. "I've been wondering who in hell Shelter Morgan was."

Proxmeyer's horse shifted uneasily, not liking the smell of smoke from the blazing house. Shelter had to shout now to be heard above the flames.

"What's going on?" he asked Proxmeyer.

"You want me to tell *you!*" The sheriff smiled thinly. "All I know is some old man with a white beard came to my office and said there was some kind of war going to happen out here. Said they had been robbed, people killed . . . he babbled some kind of nonsense about him being Texas McCall, that dead outlaw.

"I rode out a ways and next thing I meet up with Mrs. Dantworth." Shell could see Carmalita riding a black horse which she walked forward from the shadows. She was still dressed in her filmy wrapper. Her face was slack with relief. She managed a small smile.

The sheriff went on as the house sighed and a part of the roof caved in, sending up a fountain of golden sparks.

"Mrs. Dantworth said a gang of outlaws had taken over her house. Well, I didn't have a posse and was ready to turn back when she suggested rousting her cowboys out of bed. Buck was willing and here we are. It was true?" Proxmeyer asked slowly. "Dantworth was an outlaw?"

"True. Sheriff, I need a horse in the worst way."

"Dantworth?"

"That's right. Dantworth's not his real name, but I'll tell you all about that when there's time. Just now I need a horse."

The sheriff swung down without hesitation, and Morgan swung into leather, riding out of the yard as the flames stabbed up against the dark night skies, as the dark-eyed woman watched him, her broad mouth set firmly.

The moon was riding high, pale gold against the black velvet. Dabb's horse was running straight toward the border, and the outlaw was taking no trouble to cover his tracks. Shell lifted the sheriff's deepchested gray into a loping run.

He was there, somewhere on that flat expanse of desert, and this time Dabb couldn't run, he couldn't hide. This time the ax would fall.

The big gray horse moved easily under Shell, even the low, wind-rippled sand dunes seemed to slow it not at all.

Shell scanned the empty land ahead of him, standing briefly in the stirrups. There was no sign of Dabb yet, but he was there, before the hunter.

The border was five miles off, but if Dabb thought that this invisible line sketched across the desert by politicians and mapmakers was going to save him, he was sadly mistaken.

Nothing was going to save him. Nothing was going to stop Shelter Morgan who rode not alone but with a hundred ghosts, all demanding retribution.

The night was a long, moon-shadowed trail across bleak and endless desert. Shelter settled into the rhythm of the gray horse beneath him. He had no thoughts but those concerning Dabb—which way would he go? Where could he stop and make a stand? How fresh was his horse, how bad was he hit?

The rest of the universe, people, places, events, had no meaning to him. The hours passed without him realizing it. He must have entered Mexico long ago, but that was a meaningless event.

Suddenly he drew up, yanking back hard on the reins of the startled gray.

Pre-dawn gray lightened the eastern skies. The desert lay flat and dead, a moonscape. Ahead a thin curlicue of smoke rose from behind a low dune. Shelter frowned, walking the horse slowly forward.

He heard a voice call out and he reined in again.

Nothing.

There had been something odd about the voice, but he couldn't peg it. He only knew that somewhere ahead was Dabb; just over the dune someone had started a fire.

Shell swung down from the gray and, Colt in hand, he clambered up the dune, his feet sinking deeply into the sand.

He crested the dune just as the first rose-colored flush of dawn stained the eastern horizon. He had his look and then slid back down, away from the rim of the dune.

They had him.

The smoke was from the fire they had started in his belly cavity. They had taken a knife and slit him open, piled some brush in it and set fire to it. They had cut out his tongue, cut off his eyelids. Bound hand and foot to stakes he had to endure the flames devouring his flesh. He could not even cry out with agony. Only strange gurgling sounds rose from Horatio Dabb's throat as the Chiricahua Apaches slowly tortured him to death.

17.

"He tried to turn himself in, tried to tell the sheriff that he used to be this man Texas McCall, but Proxmeyer looked at the old man and shook his head. He told him he was crazy, go on your way." Carmalita dressed in a dark blue dress, lace around the collar and sleeves, looked up at Shelter Morgan who sat the big buckskin horse, his blanket roll behind his saddle.

"So what happened to Kamolay?"

"I saw him in a town suit. Him and his daughter—she looked around as if she was waiting for someone—" Carmalita smiled. "They were waiting for the stagecoach to take them to Tucson. I was told the old man wants to travel the West, talking to men of all churches. I think he wishes to give a little money here, a little there."

"Still looking for atonement."

"What?" Carmalita's dark eyes were bright.

"Never mind." Shell tilted back his hat. "What about you, Carmalita? Your husband is dead, your house burned. What will you do?"

"Go on," she shrugged. "I will bring my family up from Mexico. My husband would never allow that. I do not have my fine house anymore, but I have a ranch, no? A fine ranch with many fine cattle. Buck has told me that there is much that could be done to improve the ranch, but my husband never wished to do anything like that."

"Buck's a good man. He knows his job." Shelter looked around the broad valley, knowing that if Buck was given his head the Double D would one day be the finest ranch in this part of the country. And Carmalita—well, she would be among family and she would have a good income to the end of her days.

"You will not change your mind?" she asked, resting her hand on his thigh. "This will be a fine place, Shelter Morgan. We could be happy."

"I know it. Maybe one day I'll be back." He shrugged.

"But not now."

"No, not now. There are more of them, Carmalita. I can't expect the Indians to do all my work." He smiled thinly and took a slow, weary breath. Then he bent low out of the saddle and kissed those soft, yielding lips. "So long, Carmalita."

"*Via con Dios,*" she said quietly. Then she stood back in the shade of the trees, arms folded beneath her breasts, watching as the tall man on the big buckskin horse rode slowly northward and forever out of her life.

THE SURVIVALIST SERIES
by Jerry Ahern

#1: TOTAL WAR   **(960, $2.50)**
The first in the shocking series that follows the unrelenting search
for ex-CIA covert operations officer John Thomas Rourke to
locate his missing family—after the button is pressed, the missiles
launched and the multimegaton bombs unleashed . . .

#2: THE NIGHTMARE BEGINS   **(810, $2.50)**
After WW III, the United States is just a memory. But ex-CIA
covert operations officer Rourke hasn't forgotten his family.
While hiding from the Soviet occupation forces, he adheres to his
search!

#3: THE QUEST   **(851, $2.50)**
Not even a deadly game of intrigue within the Soviet High Com-
mand, the formation of the American "resistance" and a highly
placed traitor in the new U.S. government can deter Rourke from
continuing his desperate search for his family.

#4: THE DOOMSAYER   **(893, $2.50)**
The most massive earthquake in history is only hours away, and
Communist-Cuban troops, Soviet-Cuban rivalry, and a traitor in
the inner circle of U.S. II block Rourke's path. But he must go
on—he is THE SURVIVALIST.

#5: THE WEB   **(1145, $2.50)**
Blizzards rage around Rourke as he picks up the trail of his family
and is forced to take shelter in a strangely quiet Tennessee valley
town. Things seem too normal here, as if no one has heard of the
War; but the quiet isn't going to last for long!

*Available wherever paperbacks are sold, or order direct from the
Publisher. Send cover price plus 50¢ per copy for mailing and
handling to Zebra Books, 475 Park Avenue South, New York,
N.Y. 10016. DO NOT SEND CASH.*

THE CONTINUING MERCENARY SERIES
BY AXEL KILGORE

#8: ASSASSIN'S EXPRESS (955, $2.50)
Intrigue at every curve. That's what Frost finds while driving a
sultry undercover agent from Los Angeles to Washington, D.C.
But someone wants them off the road, and Frost has to find out
why!

#9: THE TERROR CONTRACT (985, $2.50)
Frost follows a bloody trail of killings and kidnappings when he
infiltrates a global terror network. His aim: to seek revenge on the
gang that killed his woman!

#10: BUSH WARFARE (1023, $2.50)
Hijacked in Africa, Frost awakens in a jungle and finds himself
poisoned by a deadly woman. After he gets the antidote—he plans
to give her a taste of her own medicine!

#11: DEATH LUST! (1056, $2.50)
Frost is trailing the treacherous Eva Chapman, a munitions runner
who has enough weapons to field an army. He vows to killer
her—before she plunges the world into nuclear war!

#12: HEADSHOT! (1129, $2.50)
As Frost fights against Castro death squads, M-19 guerillas, and
professional hitmen, it's hard for him to figure if the fiery beauty
who hired him wants him more as a lover—or as a target!

#13: NAKED BLADE, NAKED GUN (1162, $2.50)
When the merc runs into an old adversary—who blew away his
C.O. back in 'Nam—he's on a trail that leads to the murderously
eager arms of a group of religious fanatics—being run from
Moscow!

*Available wherever paperbacks are sold, or order direct from the
Publisher. Send cover price plus 50¢ per copy for mailing and
handling to Zebra Books, 475 Park Avenue South, New York,
N.Y. 10016. DO NOT SEND CASH.*